Edward Martyn, George Moore

The Heather Field and Maeve

Edward Martyn, George Moore

The Heather Field and Maeve

ISBN/EAN: 9783743393455

Manufactured in Europe, USA, Canada, Australia, Japa

Cover: Foto ©Andreas Hilbeck / pixelio.de

Manufactured and distributed by brebook publishing software (www.brebook.com)

Edward Martyn, George Moore

The Heather Field and Maeve

THE HEATHER FIELD

AND

MAEVE

BY

EDWARD MARTYN

AUTHOR OF "MORGANTE THE LESSER"

WITH AN INTRODUCTION BY

GEORGE MOORE

LONDON

DUCKWORTH & CO.

3 HENRIETTA STREET, W.C.

MDCCCXCIX

INTRODUCTION

In the publication of the two plays in this volume are involved many things: "Le Théâtre Libre," its echo in England, "The Independent Theatre," Ibsen, Mr George Alexander, Mr William Archer, "The New Century Theatre," the "Irish Literary Theatre," and the normal intelligence of theatrical audiences in France and England. It would be impossible—I mean that it would be impossible for me—to speak of the plays before speaking of these contiguous matters. Therefore with your permission . . .

It was for the purpose of acting the psychological drama, which seems to interest no part of the public except actors and men of letters, that the "Théâtre Libre" was founded. It had become known that many distinguished authors, without thought of supplying a popular demand, had written psychological plays. These remained in their desks unacted until the "Théâtre Libre" asked permission to act them. M. Antoine, its director, was anxious to put the taste of the public to the test, to find out whether the public was as opposed to the literary drama as managers seemed to think. The "Théâtre Libre" was imitated in England under the name of the "Independent Theatre," with this difference, that I did not hope to discover any psychological drama in England. English prose is mercenary, English dramatic prose is the most mercenary of all. I did not expect to recover literary drama from the desks of our dramatists, I knew that none was there. Before a nation can produce art it must see art, and my hope rested on the supposition that the wealthy would subscribe sufficient money to pay for a monthly performance of a work of art. That this work of art should be of British origin did not seem to me to be of immediate importance; and the money required was so little, £2000 a year or even less, £1500, would have been ample funds for the "Independent Theatre." I gave up all my time and energy to the production of the first plays produced by the "Independent Theatre." They created some passing literary interest, but little by little the truth was borne in upon me that there were not 1500 people in London who cared sufficiently for dramatic art to pay one guinea a year to save dramatic writing from the grave into which it was slipping. Having made sure of this fact I cut the "Independent Théâtre" adrift. It has long ceased to exist, and the "Theatre Libre" in France has ceased to exist too, and for the same reason.

Our dislike to good painting nearly equals our dislike to a good play, but good painting is dependent on the good taste of a very few. The pre-Raphaelite movement was kept alive by half-a-dozen men of taste; but the art of the dramatist demands a more numerous patronage, and even the little patronage necessary for the existence of an independent Theatre was not forthcoming. The public in both countries, in France and England, for some obscure reason, which it would be vain to attempt to elucidate, regards any dramatic movement outside of the ordinary scheme of the ordinary commercial theatre, not merely with the indif-

INTRODUCTION

ference which might be expected, but with a fierce hos-
tility which is incomprehensible. To many this will seem
an exaggeration, but many will remember the sullen opposition to the first performance of " The Doll's House."
It is not too much to say that to like Ibsen's plays
in the eighties was equivalent to liking Wagner's music.
Both were regarded with oblique looks, and few were
quite sure that the new music and the new drama were
not an immorality, which it was perhaps the duty of the
state to stamp out. Not infrequently this view found
expression in the writings of men who, on all other
points, were as sane and as mediocre as their fellows.
It was not until the other day that the critic ceased to
confuse the poet philosopher with a social reformer, interested in the liberation of women from their husbands,
and in the struggle between capital and labour. It has
only just come to be suspected that perhaps Ibsen did
not write his plays to prove the necessity for reformation
in these directions.

Wagner has had his revenge ; but Ibsen, though he
has ceased to be execrated, has remained unpopular ;
perhaps he has even lost adherents, for, in replying to
some admirers, he admitted that poetry interested him
more than social reformations.

In Ibsen are combined poet, philosopher and dramatist
in almost the same proportions as in Shakespeare, more
than in Racine, Goethe or Hugo. He is deficient only
in the romantic spectacle which Shakespeare provides in
abundance. Shakespeare alone amid dramatists was able to
remain a poet for his pleasure while conceding booths and
roundabouts to his audience for theirs. But the psychological drama does not admit of spectacle ; that is why

it fails on the stage. The explanation is a sad one, for if it be true we shall never possess a popular literary drama again. The psychological drama is the only possible literary drama in the nineteenth century. The romantic incidents which abound in Shakespeare were part and parcel of Elizabethan life; there was more room in the world then; at every few miles the realities of life faded to a romantic background. In the seventeenth century, duels, conspiracies, serenades and poisoned goblets were common circumstances, and could be freely used by the dramatists; they are still the stock-in-trade of the drama of the nineteenth century; they still hold the interest of sophisticated audiences anxious to be amused, but the skill of no one will ever endow them with life again. . . . Perhaps without laying ourselves open to the suspicion of believing that a theatrical audience will ever be found less unintelligent than the audiences which collect nightly in our theatres, we may wonder if this present theatrical convention will not wear itself out as the convention of Italian opera has worn out. The theatrical folk of fifty years hence, possessed by a foolish notion of progress, may decide that they do not care for scenery, dresses and romantic adventure, and welcome as a change the psychological drama which to-day is deemed pernicious and intolerable, even when written by the second greatest dramatic genius this world has seen.

In this long interval the drama will exist as a pretext for actors and actresses to dress themselves in fine clothes and to posture for the mild distraction of a public that has eaten itself into a stupor. But should a revolution in taste come to pass, will it endure? The public is the original jungle, and the garden that has been won from the jungle very soon returns to the jungle. A better chance is that some man may awake to the idea that there are others to endow hospitals and that it is his mission to endow a theatre. Until then those who write plays from impulse, because they have something to say, must publish their plays in book form. Appeal may be made to the vanity of the actor-manager and his wife; the vanity of the actor and actress is a gleam of hope in a dark outlook, a fugitive gleam.

"I have brought to you a play, Alexander, in which there is a real live man, one just born into literary life—he has never been seen on the stage—no, he is not out of a novel. But," I added, seeing his face brighten too rapidly, "there is not a penny of money in the play. It is merely a good part."

"Is it then so well written that——"

"The fault lies deeper than the writing. The public will tolerate good writing, but what it will not tolerate is, that a play should be built on a solid base of human idea and emotion, etc. . . . If the play be frivolous in its conception, the public will tolerate artifices of language."

Mr Alexander read the play and promised to produce it at a morning performance, and that he did not fulfil his promise is no part of my present grievance. A broken promise were a pitiful thing to lament. It would be no wiser to reproach Mr Alexander for having produced plays out of whose inanities he has made a fortune. He did well to produce these plays, for nine-tenths of an actor's life must be given up to rubbish; rubbish is the fare

INTRODUCTION

of the multitude, and it is the multitude that enables the actor to keep the roof over his head; but he should reserve a tenth part of his life for himself—for his art. All actors try to do this, for actors love their art; they talk about it incessantly and never about their salaries; in this respect their attitude towards their art compares very favourably with that of authors towards theirs. (When I say authors, I of course mean the members of the Society of Authors.) No one recognises the human emotions and no one welcomes them in a play more than actors, and if it were their taste that obtained, Ibsen would be the most popular dramatist. The taste of actors in plays is identical with that of the "Independent Theatre," but it is the taste of the public that obtains, and so Sardou and Cyrano de Bergerac, which is merely rhymed Sardou, are hoisted above Ibsen. The vanity of the actor impels him toward art; for six months, for ten months of the year he is forced to inhale and exhale nonsense, on the eleventh he longs to rush out of the confined and vitiated atmosphere of the theatre into the open air of art; his tired lungs pant for a breath of human emotion; and this is the moment when the dramatic author should get him to sign an agreement to produce his play. It was in such a revulsion of feeling that Mr Alexander was caught, and if he broke his promise after having made it to me, it was the fault of the dramatic critics. I will name the principal delinquent, Mr Archer, and explain.

True it is that he and I are moved by the same desire to see literature on the stage; he has given up his life, I gave up some months, perhaps a year of my life, to attain this object. I retired from the struggle, he has persisted.

xii

INTRODUCTION

Our taste in dramatic literature often coincided; our admiration of Ibsen is the same, but though our eyes were set on the same goal, the ways by which we hoped to reach that goal were different ways. My belief was that the most likely way of arriving at the goal was by an uncompromising sincerity, by taking no heed of vain appearance, by going to the root of things and denouncing all pseudo-literature in the rudest possible terms. For plays like the "Circus Girl" and "Charlie's Aunt" much toleration should be shown, but the pseudo-literature play should be held up to contempt. Mr Archer's belief was that the goal could be reached by encouraging, with insincere praise, all work that seemed new, every play that seemed better than the last play; his attitude towards dramatic writing has therefore been one of benevolent insincerity. He has pursued this policy for twenty years, and he has only to hear the plays now running at the London theatres to be convinced that he has not "educated" the public taste.

Like another he probably once believed that he had not lived in vain. The night of the production of "The Second Mrs Tanqueray" his hopes stood higher than they ever did before or since. Some years have passed, the circumstances which engendered the play are scattered, we can see it in its relation to literature and measure it by its humanities. It must be now plain to every one that it was no more than a dramatic version of the current gossip of the street. Folk were then talking of women with pasts : were asking what a man should do if he married a woman who told him that she had had a lover before she was married, and then what a man should do if he found out that his wife had had a lover before her marriage, and so on. The most astonishingly ill-devised tales were concocted by our dramatists on these themes. Mr Alexander, who likes betting on the taste of the public, produced one with success; and in the same spirit he bet on the taste of the public with a very horrible play called "The Conquerors"—and lost. But Mr Archer mistook "The Second Mrs Tanqueray" for a work of art, he declared it to be a play of the deepest social and literary significance, and the beginning of a dramatic renaissance. The actor-manager's conscience or his vanity was appeased; he was convinced against his better judgment that he had ceased to talk nonsense on the stage; he believed that he was engaged in earnest work, etc.; why, therefore, should he produce "The Heather Field"? I had admitted that I did not think it would draw money, he was agreed with me on that point; as for art, why speak of it? Had he not fulfilled his artistic destiny by producing "The Second Mrs Tanqueray"?

Actors are better judges of literature than is generally supposed, their love of the humanities from which they are for ever debarred leads them aright, but bewildered by the press, Mr Alexander for a moment seems to have thought that perhaps, after all, there was a little money in literature, and hearing that Mr Henry James had written some plays he applied for one. I would not be discourteous to Mr Henry James; perhaps the worst discourtesy would be to refrain from saying exactly what I think of his play. Speak of it I must—the explanation on which I am engaged obliges me to speak of it; and what it is needful that I should say about "Guy Domville" he knows already. He knows that it was not vulgar, like "The Second Mrs Tanqueray," but a mere hapless effort to speak in a language which he had not yet moulded to his lips. The knowledge that what he wrote was going to be spoken and not read seemed to have paralyzed his thoughts, until in the third act he could not express himself at all. In the first act some design was recognisable, but in the second and third acts everything that makes life, instinct, desire and reason, was swallowed up in flat fog. The incomparable Tourgueneff underwent the same kind of aberration when he wrote his five-act comedy, and his failure was in the same direction as Mr James's. But instead of such simple truth every kind, almost every kind, of insincerity filled the newspapers. About the construction of the story some doubt was expressed, but the writing of it could not be sufficiently praised. Did the critics look into their hearts to discover what they really thought of the writing of the play or did they say it was well written because Mr James wrote it? They were impressed by the sentences, which were elaborately composed and wore a thoughtful air. Alas, current criticism cannot understand that to think well is to write well, that an idea which has been conceived in hesitation and fear must of necessity be badly written. If the critics had looked into their hearts, if they had striven to discover their real thoughts from floating masses of preconceived opinion, they must have learnt that the play for different reasons, but for equally valid reasons, was no nearer to literature than any drama by Mr George R. Sims. Few read dramatic criticism, and it is forgotten as soon as the page on which it appears is passed. Dramatic criticism is as ephemeral as a fashion article; successful plays are but fashions; but even

INTRODUCTION

about fashions the critic is behoven to write truthfully.
We may not answer, ' what matter whether women wear
one kind of sleeve or another?' Every lie matters, and the
attitude of benevolent insincerity which the critics assumed
towards Mr James's play produced its little effect in the
subconscious mind of Mr Alexander and in the general
mind, which is always subconscious. The critical articles
which condoned instead of condemning induced a feeling
of resentment against literature, a feeling that may be
interpreted in the following words : " So that is literature !
you all say it is, . . . well, literature does not do on
the stage."

The next attempt to foster the literary play was made
by a new Society constituted probably after the fashion
of the " Independent Theatre " Society. It was called the
" New Century Theatre," and the first play that the new
dramatic society produced was Ibsen's " John Gabriel
Borkman."

To produce Ibsen was so obviously the right thing to
do that the wisdom of the management does not transpire
in the choice any more than the wisdom of the captain of
a man-of-war transpires when he fires a salute to the
Queen. To judge the wisdom of the new management
we must look to its second rather than to its first production, and the second play that the New Century
Theatre produced was a sort of sea captain's yarn of
robbery and murder, written in a language compiled very
carefully from the Bible and Scotch idiom. That Mr
Archer, the admirer of " The Second Mrs Tanqueray " and " Guy Domville " should mistake this piece
of ingenious tinkering for a work of original genius seems
natural enough if we consider how his taste oscillates

INTRODUCTION

between love of an exhibition of some social problem on one side and literary writing on the other. The difficulty is not to understand why he should like the three above mentioned plays, but why he should also like the "Master Builder." For Catholicity in art consists in admiring such different things as the sculpture of the Parthenon and that of Chartres Cathedral; but if a third admiration—let us say a picture by Sir Edward Burne Jones—be introduced, we are forced to conclude that the critic has not understood either the first or the second.

The management of the New Century Theatre was in the hands of Mr Archer, Mr Massingham, and Miss Robins; and not only did they choose a sea-captain's yarn for their second production, but they still further exposed the feebleness of their taste by selecting a one-act play to precede it, whose feebleness ranged beyond those wide bounds marked out for feebleness to range in by unpretentious suburban managements.

Mr Archer and Mr Massingham are critics of the drama. They advocate Wagner theatres and subsidised theatres, so I will say to them that it would be well to have a subsidised theatre if we had a man with a sufficiently definite taste to conduct it; a man who could admire the Parthenon and Chartres Cathedral, but who did not dally with Mr Leader or his Associate Jones. Antoine was such a man, and Mr Archer did seem once like the man who could successfully direct a literary theatre. But he likes so many things; his taste is so varied that he may be said to have no taste. He admires another Jones and praises "Michael and his Lost Angel." "The Second Mrs Tanqueray" induced him to believe that we were on the eve of a dramatic renaissance. The variations in Mr Archer's tastes are so unexpected that he has become for me what the game of "Patience" is for others. In lonely evenings it is always a distraction to try to penetrate to the secret of his nature, to discover why he likes "Hedder Gabler" and "The Benefit of the Doubt." We all play the game of "Patience" in some form or other, and the reconcilement of an admiration for "The Benefit of the Doubt" with any considerable intelligence is the problem I often set myself. And sometimes I think that it may be explained by the antagonism of the Puritan Mr Archer to the playgoer Mr Archer; the Puritan demanded atonement from the playgoer, and the atonement that the Scotch ancestor demanded was the sacrifice of all personal vanity; so Mr Archer became a dramatic critic. But the original ancestor demanded further sacrifice; and Mr Archer renounced original work and accepted the hard fare of translation. But outraged Nature has reasserted herself in Mr Archer's sub-conscious mind. He says, 'I lay no egg but I think I might hatch one.' Of all objects in Nature none is perhaps more pathetic than a clucking hen, and when the last chicken was hatched out I consented to go and see it. "He really has begun to think," said the anxious parent. "But," I said, "the thinking chicken does not begin to think, he begins by thinking."

The play was the unfortunate "Benefit of the Doubt," and the divorce court has always been accepted by Mr Archer as the symbol of thoughtfulness. . . . There is no reason why the hapless tale should be unfolded here; it matters little whether the wife confessed or the husband found her out; suffice it to say that Mr Pinero, who is about as subjective as a clown, soon began to wander round the dramatic ring hoop in hand. All the usual hoops were jumped in the second act, overheard conversations and the rest; but not one of his characters could he get through the psychological hoop; round and round they went, missing it time out of mind. The poor jester stood in the middle of the third act, a psychological and a theological hoop in either hand, tired out, the horses at walking pace, the ladies swinging limp on their wide saddles. It was eleven o'clock! There was nothing for it but to call a bishop down from the gallery to pull the performance through somehow. There were a bishop in the play and a young man called Claude, and these were the folk who did not satisfy Mr Archer. The bishop after all did bring the play to a conclusion, and Claude seemed to me one of the most amusing creations of the greatest creator of comic characters since Dickens.

No one discovered the moral of this play; perhaps it had none, but the moral of the articles that were written about it was clear enough. Again the press endeavoured to deceive the public. Mr Pinero had been put forward as a thinker; the play was rigmarole, but to admit that it was rigmarole would be to compromise for ever the literary drama. So Mr Archer thought; whereas it is by supporting such plays that the press compromises the chances of the literary drama. "Again," the public said, in its dim sub-conscious way, "if that is literature I do not like literature." And since the failure of that most dismal play indifference has settled over things theatrical: farce and melodrama and musical comedy are everywhere.

INTRODUCTION

I have to reproach Mr Archer with sins of omission as well as with sins of commission. For while he was defending the indefensible and exhausting the patience of the public with a tale of the sea, there was published unbeknown to him in London a play, beautiful as anything in Maeterlinck, a play possessing all the beauties of the Princess Maleine, and the beauty of verses equal to the verses of Homer. The name of this play is the "Countess Cathleen," and the name of its author is W. B. Yeats. If I had mentioned the name of a certain popular writer of military jargon our silly literary press would bubble with enjoyment, but the genius of W. B. Yeats, being a survival of that of the prophet and the seer of old time, escapes the appreciation of the newspapers.

That those who find the natural outlet of their lives in Newmarket and the Riviera should not have read the "Countess Cathleen" is comprehensible enough ; but that those whose life's business would seem to be to understand art, should read the "Countess Cathleen" and prefer "Admiral Guinea" and "The Benefit of the Doubt," is surely a sign of the degrading influence of newspaper criticism upon those who write it. Or shall we hazard a conjecture? Shall we say that Mr Archer has not spoken or written about this play because the English reviews are only open to chatter about the doings of little Belgians and Frenchmen? The bi-monthly article about a French poet is one of the literary conventions of our day. But even if we accept this convention as a sufficient explanation for Mr Archer's silence regarding the "Countess Cathleen," the choice of the New Century Theatre for its second production still remains unexplained. The beauty of the verses and the perfection of the construction of this play will be admitted by Mr Archer ; it will be on the character drawing that he will sharpen his pen. . . . But do we not hear too much of the differentiation of one man from another ? Is not character drawing a mere rind of life in which the English novel is still seeking an existence ? And without being thought to say that it were well to ignore social differences, may it not be suggested that they are worthy of no more than a passing notice ? Temperamental differences are more important, but even they are but the threshold of the deep regions of humanity—those states of eternal consciousness which are souls in a far deeper sense than we are souls. When the critic has said, as he says too frequently, "I do not see your hero, I do not see your heroine," he has not said everything ; he has not uttered, as he thinks he has, the final reproof. What we see most clearly is not always most real, another and a more abiding reality exists in our immortal instincts. The Countess Cathleen being a creature of myth, and stripped of all circumstantial habit, is visible only to the eyes of the soul, and represents only that which is most human and eternal in man. . . . She would barter her soul to gain the salvation of those who are selling their souls for food in famine time. But this compact is an impossible compact ; we barter our souls only for selfish gratification ; and it was the genius of the primitive poem to imagine such paradoxical sacrifice, in order to represent the blindness of human pity. A fixed idea like the Countess Cathleen looks neither to the right nor left ; she walks straight for the chasm, but instead of falling she ascends an angel to heaven, her intention being pure.

INTRODUCTION

It was open to Mr Archer, Miss Robins and Mr Massingham to have produced this divine play; or if they had wanted a prose play they might have produced "The Heather Field," which will now be performed by the Irish Literary Theatre on alternate nights with Mr Yeats' play. . . . I sent "The Heather Field" to Mr Archer, but he did not see as much as Mr Alexander saw in it, nor did discussion help him to understand that it was the first play written in English inspired by the examples of Ibsen. He seemed still involved in the traditional comprehension of Ibsen which discerns a social reformer in the greatest dramatic poet and thinker since Shakespeare, or maybe it was the man who paints from life, straight away, without troubling himself about symbolism, that Mr Archer saw in Ibsen at that time. He said, speaking of "The Heather Field" and "The Benefit of the Doubt," that it was open to me to prefer a piece of rude original sculpture to a piece of academic work. It is not required that I should raise the question whether academic work expresses qualities of balance, design, sequence. However this may be, it is certain that these qualities are as conspicuously present in "The Heather Field" as they are conspicuously absent from "The Benefit of the Doubt." A play that possesses qualities of balance, design, sequence is a work of art and will hold its own in any company; and although "The Heather Field" will seem small by the side of "The Wild Duck," it will hold its own by the side of "The Wild Duck," or "Macbeth," or "Hamlet," just as a housewife by Peter de Hoogh will hold its own by the side of the "Marriage Feast" by Veronese, or the "Entombment of Christ" by Titian, or the "Last Judg-

ment", by Michael Angelo. The little story entitled
"Ships that Pass in the Night" is not lofty in conception
nor very profound, but it is wistful and true, and it therefore holds its own by the side of "Don Quixote," "On
the Eve," and "l'Education Sentimentale." A picture
or poem that does not hold its own by the side of the
greatest works is not worthy of consideration, is not
art. Art is full of differences of style which seem to
amount to contradictions, but art is always the same, and
the true critic is he who is not deceived by the superficial
appearance. But the mission of the journalist is to record
appearances. . . . I think that in these last lines I have
made something clear that was not clear before, and it is
not impossible that many will understand now why "The
Second Mrs Tanqueray" stands beyond the pale, not being
of the right flesh and blood, while "The Heather Field"
stands well within the pale. I apologise for the words
"well within," they are unnecessary; there is no border-
land: picture, poem, statue, novel, sonata, should enter
instantly by right of birth or be thrust outside like
hirelings.

M. Jules Lemaître has published several volumes of
criticism, and so far as I remember without failing to
distinguish between the sheep and the goats. But Mr
Archer is never sure which is which, and his sins of
commission are only to be paralleled by his sins of
omission. He failed to perceive that the hero of "The
Heather Field," Carden Tyrrell, is the first appearance
of humanity in the English prose drama of to-day—
of the eternal instinctive humanities and not the ephemeral differences which divide the grocer from the
baronet. It were surely impossible to point to a

INTRODUCTION

scene in the English prose drama of the present
century so essentially human as the scene in which
Carden Tyrrell speaks to his brother Miles of the days
when they sailed their skiff to Lorlie, and Carden, who
is the elder brother, tells Miles, who was then a boy, the
legends of the Rhine. This scene is certainly a beautiful
and pathetic expression of that passionate wistfulness
which rises up in the heart and brain when we look back
on the days of our early youth, those days fresh and
fugitive as the days of early spring, when the buds are
breaking into tiny leaf and the daffodils star the
grass. In a moment we are in the midst of the
emotion which Mr Martyn has expressed in this scene,
an emotion known to all over thirty, to the hind as
well as the king. Expression of it has hitherto been
sought by bringing together an elderly spinster and an
elderly bachelor who did not marry, and who fear
that it is now too late, the assumption being that if
they had married they would have been happy. But
Mr Martyn probes deeper than the ephemeral griefs
which circumstances create, and in the scene between
Carden Tyrrell and Miles Tyrrell we are face to face with
that primal melancholy which is at the root of human
existence, we look into its eyes, infinite as the sky, and
are absorbed in pity for all things that live, and we feel in
our soul the truth that man was not intended to be happy.
This scene occurs again at the close of the third act;
in a modified form, it brings the play to its conclusion. Carden Tyrrell is a man whose dreams are in
conflict with reality. He might have lived in some quiet
library or some dim museum, happy in antiquarian re-
search, but attracted by her beauty he marries a narrow-

INTRODUCTION

minded conventional woman of the world, and his dreams, instead of being expended in art, turn to the reclamation of the Heather Field. Mortgage after mortgage is placed upon the property, and the future of his wife and child is compromised. The play resolves itself into a duel between husband and wife, and one of its merits is that although all right and good sense are on the wife's side, the sympathy is always with Carden. We forget the ruin he is bringing on his family, and we love him for his dreams, for his dreams are the eternal aspiration of man for the ideal. He hears voices, magical voices on the mountain side, and in his heart the sound of a silver harp string.

The Heather Field is the symbol of his incurable nature; whatever its circumstances it will seek its destiny out and find it; and with the flowering of the Heather Field Carden passes quietly over the border-land. The years, with all their hideous realities fall behind him, wife, domestic misfortunes and middle age, all that has been done becomes undone; his wife becomes Miss Desmond; his little son Kit becomes his brother Miles; Carden is young again and he babbles of the rainbow, of the Rhine, the gold of the Rhine and its legends; he attains his lost youth, the soft scent and colour of the spring mornings, the green leaf and the meadow starred with daffodils. "It is always morning now for me," he exclaims. The others watch him baffled and unhappy, they are still involved in the cruel coil of reality which he has shaken off, and he leads the child to see the rainbow, "that mystic highway of man's speechless longings."

Carden Tyrrell will appear to the superficial reader merely as a man who lives in a state of chronic mis-

INTRODUCTION

understanding with his wife, and squanders his fortune in experiments for the reclamation of waste land; and in Maeve the superficial reader will perceive a young lady who finds herself unable to marry the man she has promised to marry, and who is rescued from her dilemma by Queen Maeve who rises from the great cairn, and accompanied by her harpers and warriors, carries the young girl away to Tir-nan-ogue. But the discerning reader will at once understand that notwithstanding much apparent dissimilarity of subject the two plays are but different expressions of the same thought, and the power to re-tell the same story in a different form he will recognise as the sign of the true artist. The idea of both plays is that silvery beauty which survives in the human heart, which we see shimmering to the horizon, leading our longings beyond the world, and we hear it in our hearts like silver harp strings, sounding seemingly of themselves, for no hand is by. The morning light, the hoar frost, the moonlight wandering among the mountains are the natural symbols of this divine beauty. Therefore Maeve is made of moonlight and hoar frost and light of morning. We do not discover her among our acquaintances, but everyone discovers her when he wills to do so in his own heart. Maeve is a character evolved out of a place; she is made out of the light of the keen bright Irish spring and the loneliness of the Clare mountains that surround her home, of the round tower, the masterwork of Goban, on which she gazes with intense eyes; of the legends of the ancient Irish gods, of the beauty of the Irish romanesque ornament, those exquisite traceries which are a reflection of the Byzantine, but more refined.

INTRODUCTION

Maeve is the spirit and sense of an ill-fated race, and she portrays its destiny and bears the still unextinguished light of its heroic period. Maeve is all ecstasy, tremulous white ecstasy, cold as ice and glittering like ice in the moonlight. She looks beyond the world for her love; she is haunted by the herolepsy of the plume and the spear of the warrior, and sees her lover the chiefest among the chieftains of Queen Maeve. Maeve's love is a cerebral crithism which shrinks from all contact or even thought of the contact of flesh. But this severance of her temperament from the strange fruition of all our holy and most tender aspirations does not alienate our sympathy from her. Although shorn of all common humanity, our sympathy is with her as it is with Carden Tyrrell, and we cry, "Believe in your warrior of long ago, and let go by you the young Englishman who seeks to rob you of your dream;" and to triumph thus over common instincts and infect the reader with sympathies and longing which lie beyond the world is surely to succeed where hitherto no modern English dramatist has even dreamed that drama was to be found.

These plays are perfectly constructed; they could be acted as they are written, without curtailment; they were composed with strict regard for the stage, though perhaps not with a view to representation on the stage. Mr Martyn was not innocent enough to think that plays in which human emotion is the whole of the play, would be tolerated in a theatre of the present day. He wrote them with strict regard for the stage, because it is impossible to write good plays without the actors and the actresses who will never interpret them, always

INTRODUCTION

before your eyes. It is as impossible to compose literary plays that do not act as it is to compose sonnets in fifteen lines ; but by some strange irony it has come to pass that the plays which lend themselves to interpretation are the plays which are neglected on the stage and cherished in the study.

GEORGE MOORE.

THE HEATHER FIELD

A PLAY IN THREE ACTS

DRAMATIS PERSONÆ

BARRY USSHER, *a landowner, student, philosopher, &c.*

LORD SHRULE, *a neighbouring landowner.*

LADY SHRULE (LILIAN), *his wife.*

CARDEN TYRRELL.

MRS GRACE TYRRELL (*born* DESMOND), *his wife.*

KIT, *their son, nine years old.*

MILES TYRRELL, *scholar of Trinity College, Dublin, and brother of Carden.*

DOCTOR DOWLING, } *physicians.*
DOCTOR ROCHE,

The action takes place about the year 1890 *in* CARDEN TYRRELL'S *house on the West coast of Ireland.*

ACT I

SCENE :—CARDEN TYRRELL's library. On the right a door leads to the dining-room and rest of house. On the left is a large empty fire-place. At back through open glass folding-doors a small garden is visible, below which the Atlantic Ocean, flanked by a mountain at left, stretches out to the horizon. Between fire-place and folding-doors stands a writing-table with chairs on either side. At the opposite part of the room near folding-doors is a large sofa. Books in shelves line all walls. In front at the right is another table covered with papers, magazines, &c., which are likewise thrown negligently over other chairs in the room. It is a bright forenoon in the Autumn.

MILES TYRRELL, a young light-haired man of about nineteen, dressed in a blue serge suit, is seated at the writing-table in deep study with several books around him. After a pause he looks up wearily, then again bends over his books.

BARRY USSHER, a lean man of about two and thirty, of medium height, with dark hair, a short pointed beard, and dressed in a riding-costume of sombre grey, enters from garden at back.

MILES (*starting*). Ah, Barry.

USSHER (*throwing his hat and hunting-whip on the sofa*). Hallo, Miles, good morning. I see you are determined to win that gold medal at Trinity—and become one day Lord Chancellor of Ireland too, I'll be bound.

MIL. (*with a faint smile*). Lord Chancellor, indeed! I

3

shall be lucky if I can pass my examination and then find just so many briefs as will afford me a living.

Uss. Why are you so despondent? You have ability.

Mil. Perhaps—if there was an opportunity of displaying it. Oh, this is no place for work.

Uss. I know what you mean. But why not study in your room upstairs?

Mil. I might do that. Still it is not so much the interruptions. It is the knowledge of what goes on, perpetually.

Uss. Are things as bad as ever?

Mil. Yes—my brother and his wife cannot agree.

Uss. How sad it is.

Mil. Oh, if only I had a quiet house to study in like yours. You live there like a sage absorbed in your books and ideas.

Uss. I fear I also find difficulties in cultivating the tastes that are congenial to me.

Mil. Why?

Uss. You see, Miles, an unfortunate landowner must devote all his attention to keeping a little of his belongings together in these bad times.

Mil. As if you were affected by bad times—you, with that fine place here joining us, and with your unencumbered estate, and no one depending upon you. You're a lucky fellow. No wonder the luck of Barry Ussher is a by-word with the country people.

Uss. They know nothing about it.

Mil. Well, in any case you seem able to live as you please. You have always means to travel, and never want for anything.

Uss. So that is your idea of luck, Miles?

4

MIL. Well, somewhat I fancy.   Isn't it yours?

Uss. I don't think these things make much difference either way.

MIL. Oh, come, Barry, you can't expect me to believe that.

Uss. Yes, I mean that what we have on one side is taken away from the other; so the world's lots are more fairly divided than you imagine.   Our natures remain much the same at their root.   There is always the original pain.

MIL. I suppose you cynical philosophers must invent some grievance from lack of real troubles.

Uss. No, Miles.

MIL. Well, if you only knew how my brother envies your good fortune.

Uss. There are others Carden Tyrrell might envy, but he need not envy me.   By the way, where is he?

MIL. He is out—I suppose in the heather field.

Uss. Oh— (*After a short pause*) He has finished all his work there, hasn't he?

MIL. Yes, the young grass is coming up beautifully now.   Do you want to see him at once?   I can send for him.   In any case he is sure to be back soon.

Uss. That will do.   I am in no great hurry.

MIL. You have some business with him?

Uss. Well, yes.   It is about this very subject of land reclamation.   I hear he is about to raise another large loan from Government, in order to extend these operations of his.

MIL. Really?

Uss. So they told me yesterday in Dublin at the Board of Works.

MIL. When Grace hears this, there will be more troubles and disputes.

USS. Most likely.   What a pity your sister-in-law defeats all her objects by her manner towards Carden.

MIL. Oh indeed, she is very impatient with him.   Yet she is good enough in her way too.

USS. Precisely; and would probably have made an excellent wife for almost any other man; but for your brother—well, it might have been better if he had never thought of marriage at all.

MIL. What?   Surely he might have found some one to suit him.   Why should you say such a thing?

USS. (*with a frightened look*).   Why?

MIL. Yes, Barry.   But what is the matter with you?

USS. (*quickly recovering himself*).   Oh, nothing, Miles—nothing.   I merely meant to say that it would be very difficult for anyone to suit Carden.   He is a person so much of himself, you know.

MIL. Ah, it is certainly a great misfortune he ever met Grace.   And their estrangement is so extraordinary for he once used to be so fond of her.

USS. Yes, they generally begin that way.   I remember just before he became engaged he told me that he thought till then he should never marry, but that at last he had found real happiness.   They all say that, you know.

MIL. You may very well philosophise over what is past, Barry.   But why did you not then try to dissuade him?

USS. Of course I tried to dissuade him then.   I did my best.

MIL. Oh, you did, did you?

6

Uss. Yes, of course.   I warned him against the danger
of marrying a girl with whom he was only acquainted so
short a time.   I entreated him to wait a while at all
events, as he was then only twenty-one and she something younger.   But all to no purpose.   Ah, if he had
waited, he could not have failed to discover that she was
only marrying him for his means and position, and that
she did not in the least care for him.   Besides I was
certain from the first that he had no real affection or
respect for her.

Mil. Indeed ?   What made you so certain of that,
Barry?

Uss. Well, you see, Carden and I had been intimate
so long.   We had been brought up together in fact, so
that I fancy I understand him better than anyone.   The
sudden overturning of all his ideas at that time seemed to
me strange and unnatural.   He was like one bewitched.
A man's whole nature somehow does not change in a
moment.   You were too young, Miles, to know him in
those days ; but he was so ideal, so imaginative, as engag-
ing as some beautiful child who saw nothing real in the
world outside his own fairy dreams.

Mil. (*with a baffled look*).   I have memories of those
days !

Uss. They are vivid with me.   Oh, he always did *so*
fascinate and interest me.   What poetry he put into those
days of my youth — the days that are dead.   (*Pause.*)
Then to see him suddenly changed, grown even prosy
under the power of her influence, it made it impossible
for me to consider this attachment of his genuine or likely
to endure.   And has not the result proved that I was
right ?

7

MIL. I fear I must admit, Barry, that you were, alas, a reliable prophet.

Uss. Oh, I foresaw all. I knew this change could not last. The old, wild nature had to break out again when the novelty was over. It was a misfortune since he was married, but it was inevitable. There are some dispositions too eerie, too ethereal, too untamable for good, steady, domestic cultivation, and if so domesticated they avenge themselves in after time. Ah, foolishly his wife and her friends thought they were going to change Carden to their model of a young man, but the latent, untamable nature was not to be subdued. Its first sign of revolt against suppression was when he began this vast work in the heather field.

MIL. (*with a puzzled look*). Barry, I—I do not understand.

Uss. Miles, you must admit it was rather an extravagant work. He has sunk a fortune of borrowed capital in the reclamation of that mountain. Look at all the men he employed to root up rocks, and the steam ploughs, too, that have been working during these last years.

MIL. But surely he will obtain a large rent for the rich grass he has made to grow there. That ought to more than compensate for his outlay.

Uss. Meanwhile interest is accruing. The grass has not grown sufficiently for letting as yet. Then payment of rent cannot follow till long after, always supposing that it ever produces much rent.

MIL. (*surprised*). Why do you say that? Is not the land good now.

Uss. Ah, Miles, do you not know that the soil in such

places is ·very wild and untamable?   If heather lands
are brought into cultivation for domestic use, they must
be watched, they must have generous and loving treatment, else their old wild nature may avenge itself.

[*He averts his look.*

MIL. (*with mingled wonder and uneasiness*). Avenge
itself? How, Barry?

USS. Why, the wild heather may break out upon
them soon again.

MIL. Oh— (*Then eagerly*) But don't you think Carden
has given the best of treatment to the heather field?

USS. (*slowly and gently*). I do not know whether
his treatment was sufficiently kind, as farmers say here
in West Ireland.   Somehow he seemed too impatient
for the change.   He was hardly considerate enough,
perhaps, in the accomplishment of his will.

MIL. (*with dejection*). You evidently think there is
something unsatisfactory in the business.

USS. Let us hope for the best, Miles.   In any case
we ought to try and prevent him from embarking in
further schemes.

MIL. Do, Barry.   If there is one person in the world
he will listen to, it is you.   Besides you will remove a
fresh cause of quarrels with Grace : and who knows but
you may be able to do more afterwards.   Stop—I see
him coming now through the garden.

[CARDEN TYRRELL, *a rather powerfully built man
of one and thirty, with light hair, spare growth
of beard, unsteady eyes, very large forehead, and
lower part of face small, dressed negligently in a
dark suit, enters from the back.*

TYR. (*smiling*). Oh, how goes it with you, Barry? You

9

have not favoured us with visits much of late. What have you been doing ?

Uss. Well, I have been to Dublin for one thing.

Tyr. So I heard. But is it true you are reducing all your rents ?

Uss. Yes, I *have* been reducing them somewhat.

Tyr. My goodness. I suppose you will end by making the tenants a present of your property. You call me a dreamer, but it seems that I am the practical man.

Uss. (*laughing*). Oh, that does not follow at all. I consider it wiser to give a little in time, than later on to have perhaps more wrung from me by the Land Commission.

Tyr. But one should never depreciate the value of one's property. I am afraid, Barry, you are mismanaging your affairs. Have you begun yet to reclaim that bog outside your demesne, as I advised ?

Uss. No, Carden.

Tyr. There, you see. Well, a fortune is to be made by such work. You would be much better employed at it than at reducing your rents. But, my dear old Barry, there is no use in arguing with you, when you are once set upon a thing. I suppose it is because you knew I would not approve of what you are doing that you have not been to see me for so long.

Uss. Always suspicious, Carden. But, may I ask why you never come to see me ?

Tyr. You forget all I have undertaken—all my responsibilities. I have little time.

Uss. And one would think my time was of no value. Perhaps, Carden, the real reason is that I might possibly

10

not appreciate some of your undertakings and responsibilities.

TYR. (*with a swift shy glance*). Why should you think so?

Uss. (*smiling*). Oh, I don't know. I was only wondering.

TYR. But why should that prevent me from going to you?

Uss. Precisely, why indeed? I should never have thought of it, if you had not first suggested the thought.

TYR. Well, you have no reason to think anything of the kind. Just as if I could be occupied in the way you imagine.

Uss. It seems odd that you should, Carden.

TYR. Yet you have an idea all the same, that I could.

Uss. Well, to tell you the truth, I heard yesterday that you were contemplating what seems to me certainly most rash.

TYR. Oh, you did, did you? Let us hear what seems to you most rash.

Uss. It is true, is it not, that you are about to borrow another large sum of money for new land improvements?

TYR. (*somewhat confused*). Yes—it is true—well?

Uss. Well—don't you think you had better not?

TYR. Why not?

Uss. Don't you think you have done enough work—for the present, at all events? Would it not be better to wait for a time and see whether what you have already accomplished is going to be successful?

MIL. Yes, Carden, don't you think you ought to wait for a while longer?

11

Tyr. Wait? Why wait, when I know the work must be successful—nay, is already successful?

Uss. You can scarcely yet be sure of that, Carden.

Tyr. Why not?

Uss. (*rather confused*). Oh, the nature——

[*He hesitates.*

Mil. You can scarcely yet be sure of what the land is capable, you know.

Tyr. Can I not see what grass it has produced.

Uss. Yes, but will that continue?

Tyr. (*scornfully*). Will that continue? Who ever heard so absurd a question. As well ask will the air continue to bear up the birds? Will its myriad life continue to pant underneath the sea? Come—my old friend, my brother—I will not have you talk in this discouraging way and make such insinuations, as if you were indeed nothing more than mere country neighbours, who cannot understand my ideas. No, you must believe in me, and inspire me with heart.

Mil. We do believe in you, Carden—but——

Uss. We only suggest prudence.

Mil. Be prudent, Carden.

Tyr. Oh, but when you understand the matter, you will see how prudent I have been. For it was absolutely necessary to obtain this further loan unless the value of the previous one was to be destroyed.

Uss. I do not follow you. Will you explain?

Tyr. Well, you see, the drainage of the heather field has practically swamped the lands below it; so I now must necessarily drain the water off from them right down to the sea. When I have finished all that grand ramification of drains, I shall have created a whole vast tract of fertile pasture which will double the value of my property. What do you think of that? Why, I believe all you people imagine that I am working in the dark, that I do not know what I am about. But I tell you I have excellent reasons for everything I undertake.

Uss. Yes, Carden, of course—but you have borrowed a vast sum of money. Take care that the interest you will have to pay the Board of Works does not exceed your income.

Tyr. There is no danger, Barry. Have I not told you that my income must be greatly increased?

Uss. You have indeed. I can only hope most sincerely that it will be so.

Tyr. But you still seem to doubt it all the same. (Ussher *is silent*). Oh, come, Barry, this is unfriendly of you. Barry, you are a prophet of evil. Heaven grant that your doubts may be vain, else—Oh, I should be the most miserable of men. But they are vain—they are, they are—even despite your other memorable prophecy that, alas, has come too true. Ah, do you remember your warning to me ten years ago?

Uss. You mean just before your marriage? Yes.

Tyr. (*gloomily*). I wonder had that anything to do with its unhappiness. I wonder if these doubts now will bring misfortune on my present undertakings.

Uss. (*in a frightened voice*). Carden, for pity's sake stop. Don't speak like that. Forget any doubts I may have now expressed. Forget them—forget them. I was wrong ever to have interfered with my advice. Never will I do so again. No—I have not the right. See, Carden, for all I know you may succeed now. I heartily hope you will. You are determined to, and discourage-

ment might only cause you to fail. No—you must not
have a second misfortune to cast at me. Good-bye.

[He prepares to go.

Mil. Oh, Barry, do not leave us in this way. Think—

Tyr. Oh, I am sorry you should take anything I said in
that light. I did not mean, Barry, really to——

Uss. No, Carden, forgive me, but I was for the
moment unnerved by the thought that you should attri-
bute to me any of your ill luck. No—I hope you will
always find me a help to you instead, whenever you may
require me.

Tyr. Ah, now you are like yourself again—the Barry
of other days. I knew you would understand me when I
explained everything to you.

Uss. I hope, Carden, at least I may never be to you
the cause of ill luck. *[Exit at back.*

Tyr. Dear old Barry, it makes him positively angry
to see me improving my property, because he has not the
enterprise to improve his own. But I think I have
convinced him that he was mistaken in his estimate of
my work.

Mil. You certainly frightened him, Carden. I have
never seen him as he was just now.

Tyr. Oh, I really did not mean what I said. He
only annoyed me by his stupid doubting.

Mil. Still—as a matter of fact long ago he tried to
dissuade you from marrying Grace—isn't that so?

Tyr. Yes. He was full of doubts and objections then
as now—only then he was right. But now—ha, ha—
well, I know he is altogether wrong.

Mil. Why do you say you know, Carden? Why are
you so certain now?

14

TYR. Because I see so clearly before me.

MIL. That at least is a comfort. But perhaps he might be wrong in the other matter too. Don't you think it would be well also if you would determine to belie his doubts of long ago as well as of to-day?

TYR. What do you mean?

MIL. Why, Carden, to try and prove that after all he was wrong when he advised you not to marry Grace.

TYR. (*with a sigh*). Ah—impossible.

MIL. Don't say that, Carden.

TYR. Oh, Miles, you do not understand.

MIL. But have you never tried?

TYR. Tried—?

MIL. Yes, tried. You know there is nothing really wrong about her.

TYR. Nothing, nothing—and everything. The same thing that is wrong about me. That is how it is between us.

MIL. But might you not try to fall in just a little with her ways? She is good after all.

TYR. My dear Miles you don't know what you are talking about. Of course she is good enough. I know that perfectly well. But she has no sense of compromise —no consideration for me at all. She always despised me.

MIL. Oh, Carden, no——

TYR. Oh, but yes. That is why she is so indignant I should take an interest in anything except herself. She would shape my life altogether after her own standard and that of Lady Shrule. I have often given in before, but the result was she became more and more exacting, until at last I found matters quite intolerable. Oh, it

15

is useless to deny that here at least Barry's warnings have come true.

MIL. How extraordinary that you should have changed so towards her—you who once were so devoted.

TYR. Ah, Miles, I have simply found her to be absolutely different from what I once imagined her. I was very young then, very inexperienced. I longed for sympathy, and thought it was easy to find. I idealised women in those days. I believed that they were idealists. Ah, that was my fatal error.

MIL. But surely you don't mean to deny that some are ?

TYR. I don't believe any are, really. They may be on an average more fanciful than man, but your true idealist can only be a man. Alas! had I known that then, my fate would have been very different. I thought others were easy to find, in whom I could confide as in Barry.

MIL. Do you consider him an idealist ?

TYR. I should think so indeed—a true idealist—only he is in a way so drilled and careful, that he will never let himself go. But he is such a friend, and understands everything. No, I never knew isolation when we were together in our youth. Isolation only began with my marriage which led me out into a lonely world. Oh, it was a great misfortune. And I have no one to blame but myself.

MIL. And yet—and yet were you really so much to blame ? She was so beautiful——

TYR. Ah, you have said it. There you have found the cause of all the trouble. But Barry would never have wavered.

16

MIL. Oh, he is a hardened philosopher whom no beauty could soften.

TYR. That is because, unlike most people, he can see the truly beautiful, and so is heedless of shams.

MIL. Shams? And you can speak like that of her beauty. How I remember her on your wedding-day, when as her little page I held her train? I was only nine years old then, and thought she was some tall white fairy that had come to live with us. Oh, Carden, think of that time. Its memory might banish much bitterness.

TYR. Too late, too late. You are still very young, Miles. I have outgrown the capability of such sentiment.

MIL. But you have not outgrown the great kindness of your nature. No, that I could never believe. Ought it not in these difficulties to help you? Why, see how good you are always to me.

TYR. Ah, yes, that is different, Miles.

MIL. And Kit, too—are you not most affectionate and kind to him?

TYR. My poor little son, of course—how could I be otherwise to him? He is really so loveable and such a companion to me. For just now he is wonderfully like what you were, Miles, when you acted as that pretty page. His age besides is the same as yours was then; so that the very sight of him calls back to me the days of my youth. Oh, that happy time before my fatal mistake! Miles, *do* you remember that time?

MIL. Remember? How well I remember!

TYR. I suppose I had troubles then, as now; but memory has idealised those past scenes, till only their beauty remains, wafted back to me like an aroma from

B   17

some lost paradise. I feel I shall never know the joy of those days again.

MIL. You must not think such things, Carden. Days as good as these will, I am sure, return.

TYR. Ah no, Miles — their poetry, never—the hope that shines like a spring-day sun upon our youth! It warms us with such life. It inspires us to attempt so many deeds. With what expectations we travel. What materials we are to make out of it all. Do you remember when we went abroad together?

MIL. (*joyfully*). Oh, yes, of course I do, Carden.

TYR. Well, it seems funny that I should have taken you with me then on travels you were too young to appreciate : but I could not bear to leave you who had no protector save me after our father died.

MIL. You kind brother.

TYR. Yes, I carried you off, my little Miles, as you were then.

MIL. And how I enjoyed myself.

TYR. What fairie towns we came to—Boppart on the Rhine with its quaint old houses. Then we sailed our boat through the hills to Lorlei, and watched where the river nymphs used long ago to glide, laughing, through the gold-lit depths of the stream.

MIL. Yes, and you told me the legend of their gold—how it was robbed and restored and still guarded by them.

TYR. I did; and you, little practical man that you were, you bent down to the water expecting to see the glitter of the Rhine Gold !

MIL. (*laughing*). The marvellous seemed real in those days.

TYR. Ah, those bright happy days! And do you remember that Sunday morning in Cologne Cathedral when all the boys sang Palestrina so divinely?

MIL. I remember we stood by great iron gates. I looked up in your face and wondered why it shone through its tears.

TYR. How pure the silver voice chords soared to the vaults of stone! Pure as our joy in those days. Fit music for those bright young days.

MIL. Yes, everything seemed joyful then.

TYR. Oh, what brave times we used to have together. You know we were always such friends.

MIL. (*with emotion*). Indeed we always were, Carden. There is no one in the whole world I love as well as you. You have ever been the best of brothers to me.

TYR. (*goes over mysteriously to* MILES). Then you think, Miles, you will always help me?

MIL. (*surprised*). Why, Carden, of course——

TYR. (*with anxious intensity*). You will not leave me, if—if ever I should stand helpless and alone, will you Miles?

MIL. Good gracious, no. But what makes you imagine such a thing?

TYR. Well, somehow I feel that persons and objects are receding from me and becoming more unreal in these later times. (*Crosses over to sofa at right and kneeling on it with one knee, gazes out at the mountain.*) Do you know, Miles, I often think that my life of pain and unrest here is only a dream after all.

MIL. And like a dream this suffering will pass away, Carden, let us hope never to return.

TYR. (*sadly*). No, oh no. It would be too much to

19

expect that. A dream—a bad dream (*as if suddenly illumined*), yet with intervals too of wakefulness now and then.

MIL. (*approaching him*). Of wakefulness? What do you mean? When are those intervals?

TYR. When I am out in the heather field.

MIL. The heather field?

TYR. (*with enthusiasm*). Yes—the great mountain field out there (*points out at back*), that it was my ideal to bring to fruitfulness. There I awaken to true life indeed, as I stand looking over the Atlantic; and sea winds sweep against my feet the young grass in its matchless Irish green that gleams a golden green in the Autumn sun to-day. There I am haunted by those departed joys of my youth—again and again.

MIL. (*with a puzzled look*). There? But why there, Carden. Why there more than anywhere else?

TYR. Oh you matter-of-fact Miles—still the same as the little wise Miles of long ago, who used to ask such quaint questions. How different we are? Yet how delightful I always find you. "Why there?" you ask. Ha, ha!

MIL. (*a little disconcerted*). Evidently you consider it a superfluous question. But I think I may very reasonably ask it all the same.

TYR. Well, then, because there after years of joyless stagnation I find myself again in an ideal domain—away from fretful surroundings—alone! except for little Kit who loves the mountain and its wild flowers. You know, Miles, how like I have said he now looks to what you were in the old days? At moments, indeed, I can hardly believe it is he and not you. So his presence there

20

is no hindrance to that evocation of the past. No ;
he serves rather to quicken the magic of the heather
field.

MIL. (*with sudden emotion*). Oh, to think I could
ever have been so much to you. How good you always
were to me, Carden.

TYR.. I could not help it. You belonged to the beauty
of that time.

MIL. All this sounds like the marvellous tales you used
to tell me when I was a child. I see your imagination is
the same as ever.

TYR. And you call what I tell you only imagination.

MIL. Well, Carden—but what else.

TYR. (*resignedly*). Ah, I suppose I cannot help you.
You too are like Barry who said the same thing when I
once told him of the voices——

MIL. (*with vague alarm*). Voices, Carden ? Why—
what now are these ?

TYR. Out there—over the mountain. Oh, the vivid
brightness of those voices, as they float back from the
past on each changing breeze !

MIL. (*anxiously*). You only heard the wind whistle
along the coast. Don't heed it any more, Carden.

TYR. Why should I not heed such celestial song ?

MIL. A dream phantom of the desolate mountain.

TYR. No ; it is only your words I hear as in a troubled
dream.

MIL. (*gently*). Carden, it is deceiving you—this
wonderful imagination.

TYR. What ?—imagination again ?

MIL. Of course.

TYR. (*patiently*). Ah well, I cannot convince you,

21

Miles. But what does it matter? You are delightfully sympathetic to me all the same. I feel this opening of my soul to you has even done me good. Yes, it does me good to be listened to occasionally. It leaves a great peace after it; and I have not felt so peaceful as now for many a day. Indeed, if this could last, it would be almost like the old time again.

[MRS GRACE TYRRELL, *a rather tall, thin woman of about thirty but looking younger, with a pale face, brown hair and an undefinable attractiveness in her outward manner and movements enters by door at R. She is dressed plainly, but with exceeding neatness.* TYRRELL *takes a large book from the shelves at back of sofa on which he then sits and turns over the leaves, suppressing a look of annoyance.*

MIL. (*going towards her politely*). I suppose you have been out on your rounds this morning as usual, Grace?

GR. Yes, as usual. Have you been here since breakfast?

MIL. Yes.

GR. Studying, I suppose.

MIL. Not much.

GR. Why?

MIL. Oh, Barry Ussher was here, and then Carden and I have been talking.

Gr. And so your morning was wasted, Miles?

MIL. Oh, not wasted, Grace.

GR. I think it would have been more profitably employed in working for your examinations than in talking to your brother.

MIL. I am not at all so certain you are right.

GR. You must admit you have plenty of time for

22

talking without allowing it to interfere with your studies.

TYR. (*looking up from his book*). It is so hard for us, Miles, is it not, when we are together, to refrain ?

GR. What you two can have to say perpetually to each other puzzles me. You never visit anywhere nor seem to know what is going on in the neighbourhood.

TYR. If we did, I am certain we shouldn't trouble to speak about it.

GR. Oh, indeed.

TYR. No ; the subjects that mutually interest us are far different. Among other things, we were talking before you came in over our journey long ago on the Continent. (*Then as if carried away by the subject of the moment*) Look, in this architectural book there are plates representing some buildings we saw then. Here is a Romanesque house at Boppart on the Rhine. It is a unique specimen of domestic architecture in that period. And here—this is the bishop's house at Würzburg. How beautifully the oriel is poised there at the angle, like a hooded falcon on its perch ; what a genius these medieval architects had for soothing with picturesque ideality the restless suffering spirit of their time. To gaze on their work makes one forget oneself and everything else——

GR. (*who the while has been looking about her with an impatient and wearied expression*). Goodness me, what a litter the room is in with all these books and papers.

TYR. (*with a momentary look of humiliation*). Oh !

GR. What brought me here, by the way, was to tell you that I must have it thoroughly dusted and tidied at once, as the Shrules come to lunch to-morrow.

23

Tyr. Yes, but what have they got to do with my room?

Gr. We shall want it to sit in. I could not think of letting anyone see it in its present state.

Tyr. (*fretfully*). Can't you leave my room alone?

Gr. There! as usual, you are disagreeable when your wife wants anything.

Tyr. No; but I have a quantity of important papers that it would give me endless trouble at present to sort, and put away.

Mil. Oh, why cause him all this inconvenience, Grace? Will not the drawing-room suit you just as well?

Gr. Lord Shrule has had an attack of gout and does not like going upstairs——

Mil. Then bring them here. But you need not upset the room. Everyone knows it's a work-room.

Gr. I could not think of allowing any strangers to see it in this state.

Mil. I wonder how you can attach so much importance——

Gr. (*coldly*). That will do, Miles. As usual you don't know what you are talking about.

Mil. Hei-ho.

[*He begins to gather his books together on the writing-table.*

Tyr. You are not going, Miles, are you?

Mil. I think I shall try if I can read in the summer-house outside.

[*Exit at back, carrying with him his books.*

Gr. (*quietly*). Well, I suppose you had better put away all these old papers at once, and let the housemaid come in.

Tyr. Impossible.—I am too busy.

24

GR. That's what you always say.   You imagine yourself the busiest man in the world ; and as a matter of fact
you have nothing to do.

TYR. Nothing to do ?

GR. (*calmly*).   What have you to do ?

TYR. (*checking his irritation*).   Very well, we won't
discuss that old subject.   Anyhow I require my papers,
as a man comes to see me to-morrow on business con-
nected with them.

GR. Who is this man ?

TYR. The drainage inspector of the Board of Works.

GR. Indeed !   Why, I thought he had finished everything here long ago.

TYR. Oh, so he has.

GR. Well, what is he coming for now ?

TYR. (*vaguely*).   Oh—you see—it would take too long
to explain just at present.   Besides you might not understand.

GR. (*with a penetrating look*).   You know I would
understand well enough.   But you never were a person
to be relied upon !   You are now trying to hide something
from me.   Come, it is as good to tell it to me at once.

TYR. (*bridling up*).   I am not trying to hide anything
from you.   I don't care whether you know it or not.

GR. Well, then, why is this man coming ?

TYR. He is to lay out some drains in the valley beneath
the heather field.

GR. (*astounded*).   What ?—You don't mean to say you
are going to drain all that immense tract of land too ?

TYR. Yes.   It is necessary now after the other work.
So I am going to obtain a new loan from Government to
carry it out.

25

GR. A new loan! We shall certainly be ruined this time.

TYR. No—no— Why, can you not see the enormous improvement this work must be to the estate?

GR. Oh, that is what you are always saying; and the estate for some years past has been steadily growing worse and worse, until now we are almost reduced to difficulties.

TYR. You are quite mistaken. I tell you we are on the eve of seeing one income doubled. Just consider the rent that must soon be produced by the heather field.

GR. (*with a gesture of impatience*). The heather field. Up to this, indeed, it has been nothing but a gigantic loss. And who knows but it may never be anything else? My goodness, can you not wait to see if it will be a success before you swamp the estate with this new debt?

TYR. No—no—every delay is a loss of profit. You do not understand.

GR. Oh, I am tired of your always telling me that I do not understand. I understand perfectly that you are bringing us to beggary.

TYR. Well—it is certainly amazing that you should think so. But then, you know, you are never open to reason—never in sympathy with my ideas.

GR. How on earth can I be, when like everyone else I believe you to be utterly mistaken in what you are doing?

TYR. I do not mean what I am doing at present—but the whole tenor of my life and ideas. You have never understood them.

GR. (*sharply*). Look here, it's beginning to irritate me

this talk about my not understanding.   So I see—you think yourself the great incomprehensible, ha, ha.   Well, you are quite mistaken.   Everyone understands you.   So do I, absolutely.   For in spite of all your efforts to be . singular, you are a very ordinary person, in whom there is nothing particular to understand.

TYR. (*helplessly*). What on earth do you mean by always harping on my efforts to be singular?   Heaven knows I cannot see how I try to be so.

GR. (*with a little laugh, as she taps her foot on the floor*). I suppose you are now habituated to the effort.

TYR. (*looking at her with a sort of wonder*). Oh, how impossible it is for you ever to know how I have suffered —how I have aspired!

GR. (*impatiently*). Really, it becomes too provoking when you begin talking about these imaginary sufferings and aspirations of yours.   What on earth have you to suffer?   You are in good health are you not?   Were you not more than fortunate to have married as you did?   Have you not independent means?   What then can a man like you aspire more to?   It is true, of course, that you have crippled your resources by mismanagement and extravagance.   But, if you will now be led by me, and put this new scheme of drainage out of your head, and if we are economical for a while, the property must recover.   Then you can have absolutely nothing to trouble you.

TYR. Oh, this matter-of-fact way you have of looking at things!   This simple barren prose of your mind!   It is that, that is driving me mad.

GR. Driving you mad——

[*Pause, during which they look at each other.*

TYR. Well, I suppose you think I am so. (*He waits*

27

for her answer.)   What an absurd idea.   This is another means of annoying me.

GR. I must defend myself.

TYR. What do you mean?

GR. Seeing you are so bent on ruining our child and me, I can only think one thing.

TYR. That I am mad?

GR. (*without answering him walks to back*).

TYR. Grace.

GR. (*turning*). Well—what is it?

TYR. Do you mean this?

GR. (*still walking to back*). What did I say?

TYR. You said—I mean you insinuated that—I am mad.

GR. (*Does not answer.*)

TYR. You do not mean this. Take back what you have said.

GR. (*turning suddenly*). I cannot.

> [*She still walks to back.*

TYR. Before you go take back your words. You don't know how they frighten me. Again I beseech you to take back those words. You do not believe what you say.

GR. I do believe them. I believe you to be mad.

> [*Exit at back.*

TYR. (*laughing nervously*). Oh—ha—mad. How can she say such a thing? Mad—who is saner than I am? Ha—ha—I suppose people of her type think everyone who differs from them, mad. How curious! Ah, we have not a single sympathy. That is what it is. (*With a look of terror*) Merciful heaven, is it possible, though, she may be right? Can there possibly be a doubt as to

28

which is the reality and which is the dream? Oh, horror
—horror! [*He sinks upon the sofa and covers his face
with his hands.*

MILES TYRRELL, *carrying his books as before, enters
at back.*

MIL. It is rather chilly reading out of doors. As I saw
Grace just go through the garden, I may perhaps again
have this place to myself. (*Perceiving* Tyrrell.) Oh, you
here still. Why, Carden, what is the matter with you?

TYR. (*rising, approaches in a dazed manner, and seems
involuntarily to feel his way with his hands*). Nothing—
only that persons and things now more than ever seem
strangely to recede from me and become more unreal. But
you—*you*, Miles, said you would never leave me (*glances
around with a shudder*) if ever I should stand helpless
and alone. Oh, Miles, my brother—

[*He hides his face on Miles' shoulder.*

MIL. Carden—

[*The books fall from his arms on the floor.*
(*End of Act I.*)

ACT II

SCENE:—The same as last, except that the room is tidied,
the window doors at back are closed, vases of flowers stand
on the tables from which the papers, &c., have been removed
and replaced by sundry drawing-room ornaments. It is the
afternoon of the following day.

MRS GRACE TYRRELL opens the door at right for LADY
SHRULE, a plain, fashionable-looking woman of about five-
and-thirty, in a riding habit and straw hat which fit her to
perfection. She enters somewhat jauntily.

GR. (*following her*). I thought we might as well sit
here after lunch instead of in the drawing-room. I know
Lord Shrule is not very fond of going upstairs.

LADY S. No ; my husband, dear old man, finds it trying after his attack of gout. Well, upon my word, Grace, this is quite a pretty room. What a pity not to turn all these frowzy books out of it.

GR. (*sighing*). Oh, of course, it ought to be a drawing-room.

LADY S. Then why don't you make it one ?

GR. My goodness, Lilian, you know I can do nothing in this house.

LADY S. I know you have a wretched time of it, dear, with that husband of yours. Still I cannot help thinking that if, at the beginning, you had really tried, you might have made him more amenable.

GR. That sounds very easy. You have no idea what he is.

LADY S. Oh, nonsense, Grace. Most men have notions before they marry : but they are soon brought to their senses, if their wives are clever. And you are clever : so that is why I say you cannot have tried.

GR. I have tried everything, Lilian, although you won't believe it.

LADY S. What—everything ?

GR. Yes.

LADY S. There is one thing I am sure you have never tried.

GR. (*eagerly*). What is that ?

LADY S. Flattery.

GR. Lilian, don't be silly. As if there was anything I could flatter him about.

LADY S. Well, you know, in spite of all, people *do* say he is clever.

GR. (*impatiently*). I must say I have never found him so.

LADY S. I confess I never have either. But then I
don't see very much of him. To tell you the truth he
always seemed to me odd and ridiculous : for he never
cared for society, never went to races, dances, or tennis
parties, you know, like other people. Still it might be
worth your while to do as I advised, You can hardly
imagine what effect it has even on the most unpromising
men.

GR. That may be, that may be, when they are really
superior to one ; but to flatter him—ugh—never (*half
to herself as she turns away*). Besides it is impossible
after yesterday.

LADY S. (*pricking up her ears*). Yesterday? What
happened yesterday, Grace?

Grace is silent.

LADY S. (*goes up to her*). What is the matter, dear ?

GR. (*petulantly*). Oh, nothing, Lilian. I did not mean
you to hear.

LADY S. Oh, but there *is* something, Grace. I see it
by your troubled look. He must have done something
dreadful yesterday. Perhaps I might be of help to you.
What was it ?

GR. Well this. Yesterday I discovered that he has
embarked on a new folly which must end in our ruin ; and
when I tried to remonstrate with him he would not listen
to a word I said.—Just think, he—he——

LADY S. He must be a great savage. But what else
can you expect from the life he leads ?

GR. Quite true. You are perfectly right, Lilian.

LADY S. What is this new folly you say he has embarked on, Grace?

GR. Oh, a monstrous plan of draining another immense

31

morass. As if our means were not already sufficiently crippled by his extravagance in this way.

LADY S. I should think so, indeed. What a misfortune for you that you ever married him.

GR. Yes—what a misfortune!

LADY S. I have always wondered why you did, Grace. You know you never cared for him. How, indeed, could any girl care for such a man—least of all the Grace Desmond I remember in those days, when we used to meet at every party and ball in the county.

GR. Yes, yes, Lilian, I know that. But you see he was a good match at the time; and I thought I would be able to make him sensible, and to lead him;—for he *was* so much in love with me.

LADY S. Was he ever really, do you think?

GR. Oh, I think so: he must have been at first; for then it seemed to me that I used to monopolise all his attention.

LADY S. How came he to change? Some other woman, I suppose—

GR. No—no. There is no one else. I am sure of that. I have watched him closely now for some years.

LADY S. Nonsense, dear—just as if *you* could watch him. I tell you it is impossible that a man can exist without loving some woman.

GR. Yes—I know we women all think so. But this is quite a case in itself. He is such a queer creature. You cannot imagine how strange his ideas are. (*With a certain relief and confidence.*) Oh, no—there is no one else; and it is very wicked of you, Lilian, to suggest such a thing.

LADY S. (*a little nettled*). How then, do you account for his behaviour?

GR. I cannot think, for I have always been most amiable to him and patient with his eccentricities, which are dreadfully irritating. Gracious, I remember when he first began to weary me with his strange ideas that I could not make head or tail of. (So you may be sure, dear, they were sheer nonsense.) It was then, when I tried to draw him from such folly, and to centre his interest upon myself, that I noticed a curious change in him. It seemed all at once that I became as nothing to him—that what he loved was something mysterious—beyond me.

LADY S. Ah, he never loved you, Grace. I am certain, now, he never did.

GR. Oh, yes, he must have at first. You should have seen how I made him do almost anything for me. Why, he settled down, entertained, shot, even farmed. Imagine that for him.

LADY S. (*composedly*). Well—what was the result? What about the farming, for instance?

GR. (*crestfallen*). Indeed—the only result of the farming has been—the heather field.

LADY S. Ah, Grace, for all you made him do, you were not able to make him give up the heather field—my poor Grace!

GR. (*with violent emotion*). Oh, that folly! That abominable work! With the beginning of it I noticed his first change towards me.

LADY S. He never loved you, Grace. He is a terrible man. These Tyrrells were always a queer lot. You know the father was very eccentric; and the mother—well, Shrule tells me she went quite out of her mind before she died, at the birth of the young brother. What

C   33

kind is he, by the way? He is very good-looking, don't you think?

GR. Oh, Miles is all right. He is a harmless creature, —wonderfully clever at college, I hear. He is certainly amiable, but vexes me occasionally with his foolish admiration for my husband.

LADY S. Yes, I can imagine how annoying that must be.

GR. Yes, and to have that fellow Ussher, too, dropping in to complete the mutual admiration society! Oh, I always disliked him.

LADY S. I don't think much of him either, with his sad, lonely way of living there in that great place of his. I believe he has it filled with such strange things.

GR. Yes, books and hideous pictures. I have not been there for years. I avoid him as much as possible; for he was always my enemy, and does his best to destroy whatever influence I might have with my husband.

LADY S. My poor Grace, what a strange crew you have fallen among! This dreadful husband! So at last he is going selfishly to sacrifice you for the gratification of his theories and whims.

GR. (*with determination*). He shall not sacrifice me, Lilian. I am certain of that now.

LADY S. Why, dear, what are you thinking of?

GR. All those facts you have mentioned about the Tyrrells only confirm a suspicion that has haunted me for some time.

LADY S. (*with increasing curiosity*). What suspicion, Grace?

GR. That my husband is not in his right senses.

LADY S. Do you mean you think him mad?

GR. Yes—mad.

LADY S. Oh!

GR. Yes, Lilian; I feel there can be no doubt about it now.   You know his monstrous extravagance, his wild manner of talking—and then what you tell me about his father and mother.—Oh, he must certainly be mad.

LADY S. I suppose you are right.

GR. Of course—that is what it is—poor man! Measures ought therefore to be taken at once to prevent him from ruining his family.

LADY S. What measures can you take, Grace?

GR. I don't see why I should not commence a legal suit to deprive him of control over the property.

LADY S. But that would mean placing him under restraint, wouldn't it?

GR. I suppose so, if necessary.   All I know is that I am determined to prevent this new burden from being put on the estate.

LADY S. Wouldn't it be well, Grace, if you were first to have medical advice as to the state of your husband's mind?

GR. I have already thought of that, Lilian.   I have been in communication with Doctor Dowling and Doctor Roche.

LADY S. What—really?

GR. Yes.   I believe two doctors are required, are they not, in cases of this sort?

LADY S. I don't know: but we can ask Shrule.

GR. Of course: he is sure to know.   How lucky I have you both here.

LADY S. When do you think of sending for the doctors?

Gr. Well, Lilian, the sooner the better, if this government loan is to be stopped. (*Hesitating*) Well, the fact is I—I have sent for them to-day.

Lady S. To-day?

Gr. Yes. Was I not right?

Lady S. But your husband suspects nothing of this?

Gr. Good heavens, no! Neither do the doctors as yet. No—I have sent for them upon the plea of their holding a consultation about Kit. As Doctor Roche has been attending him lately off and on for little attacks of feverishness and nausea, their visit will not look in any way suspicious. I will then take care they have conversation with my husband. You see?

Lady S. What energy and resource you have, dear, to be sure.

Gr. Ah, when a woman is reduced to such desperate straits as I am at present, it sharpens her wits. But the doctors may arrive now at any moment, and as I must see and prepare them beforehand for this task, let us go out to the end of the shrubbery where we can meet them on their way.

Lady S. Very well—and you can bring Shrule to join in our consultation afterwards, when he comes from the dining-room.

Gr. What a comfort, Lilian, to have you both to consult. (*Vehemently*) You must help me. I tell you I must succeed in this undertaking. It means the very existence of my child and me.

Carden Tyrrell *enters hastily at the back.*

Tyr. Oh, have you finished lunch so soon? How do you do, Lady Shrule? (*They shake hands*). I hope you

36

will excuse my absence. I was very busy all the morning with the Board of Works inspector.

LADY S. Oh, not at all.   Have you finished your business ?

TYR. No—but I expect to by to-night.   The inspector has gone in before me to lunch—so, with your permission, I will leave you to look after him.

LADY S. Of course, Mr Tyrrell—we will excuse you. Grace and I were just about to take a stroll around the garden.   You will find Shrule in the dining-room.

[*Exeunt* LADY SHRULE *and* MRS GRACE TYRRELL *at back.*   CARDEN TYRRELL *gazes after them as they disappear in the garden, then goes to writing table where he searches for something which he cannot find, while he grumbles indistinctly.   He looks around the room with an expression of annoyance at its altered condition, then exit by door at right.*

Enter at back BARRY USSHER *and* KIT TYRRELL, *a rather wild though pensive-looking boy with short, fair hair, and dressed in a sailor suit.   He has a daisy chain swung across his shoulder, and holds a bunch of wild flowers in his hand.*

KIT. (*dragging* USSHER *by the sleeve*). Come in, Barry, come in.   I missed you yesterday.   Have you brought me anything this time ?

USS. I am afraid nothing this time, Kit.   You see, when I left home I did not intend to come here ; but on the road I met by chance Doctor Roche, who told me he had been sent for by your mother.   So I thought I would just turn in, and see if anything was the matter.   There is no one ill, is there ?

37

KIT. No, of course not. They are only bringing him to bother me again. I have nothing the matter with me; and still he is always saying I must not eat this and I must not eat that.

USS. What a nasty old fellow!

KIT. Yes—isn't he horrid? He says, too, I mustn't lie on the grass. I suppose he'll soon want to prevent me hunting for wild flowers.

USS. That *would* be a privation, Kit. You love them so much, don't you? What nice ones you have brought in to-day. Where did you get them—so late, too, in the year?

KIT. Oh, you can't·think how I had to search for them here and there through the long grass in the heather field. It is the only place now where any wild flowers are left. How I love being there with father.

USS. So you, Kit, have also caught the sickness of the heather field.

KIT. What is this sickness you are all saying I have? I tell you I am quite well. (*With impatience*) Oh, how I wish I were a man.

USS. Alas, are you not much better as you are? Why do you want to be a man?

KIT. Because then they could not prevent me doing what I like. I should be a sailor and find out what is beyond that great sea father and I are always looking at from the heather field.

USS. Be a sailor, Kit, and give up the wild flowers?

KIT. Oh, I forgot. But should I have to, do you think?

USS. I fear you could not gather flowers on the sea,

38

except, perhaps, a few poor crushed ones, torn from its depths by the storms.

KIT. Then there *are* some, after all?

USS. Yes—down under the sea grow numberless fair flowers whose leaves close softly around many a poor sailor.

KIT. (*dreamily*). What beautiful flowers!

USS. I hope you will never be such a sailor, Kit. No, you are far better as you are! Do not wish to be a man.

KIT. Why, Barry?

USS. Because you understand so many things now you never could then. How much nicer to be always a little wildflower elf! In the lives of dream children such as you it is beautiful to think of a heather field.

KIT. Oh, but can they prevent me from going there?

USS. They cannot. I will see that old Roche attempts no such tyranny.

KIT. Oh, thank you, Barry. How good you always are!

LORD SHRULE, *an elderly benevolent-looking man dressed in a somewhat old-fashioned riding costume,* MILES TYRRELL, *and* CARDEN TYRRELL *enter by the door at right.*

LORD S. Now that the inspector has gone out again to his work, I must say, my dear Carden, I am astounded at hearing of this new expenditure you contemplate. I did not like to speak before him— Ah, Ussher, how do you do? (*To* KIT) And how is my little man?

KIT. (*holding out his hand*). Very well, thanks.

LORD S. That's right, that's right. I was saying, my

39

dear Carden, your fresh project of expenditure fills me with amazement.   Have you heard about it, Ussher?

Uss. I have indeed.

Lord S. Well, does it not seem to you extremely imprudent—nay, reckless?

Uss. Oh, you must not ask me, Lord Shrule.   Carden seems determined.   And, after all, he is the best judge of his own affairs.

Tyr. Yes, Barry, that is just it.

Lord S. Come, come, Carden, you will not mind the advice of an old man who has a long experience in the management of land.   Your father and I were always fast friends, and I naturally take a great interest in you and your family.

Tyr. I know you have always been very kind, Lord Shrule.   Forgive me if I have spoken hastily.   I did not mean—

Lord S. Of course not, my dear Carden.   I quite understand you.   I fear indeed you must think it rather impertinent of your friends to interfere in your business.   But then, as I have said, I consider myself privileged.

Tyr. You may be quite sure, Lord Shrule, I could not take anything from you except in good part.

Lord S. I thought so.   Well, let me implore of you, if only for the sake of your family, to desist.   This is certainly the wildest scheme I ever . heard of, and couldn't pay, even if the drainage were to turn out a success.

Tyr. But you forget it is necessary now that the drainage of the heather field falls into this land.   I *must* make a cutting for the water to get to the sea.   And then, what is easier than to reclaim the land through which this cutting goes?.

LORD S. My dear Carden, don't mind the cutting—don't mind the heather field. What you have only got to think of is to cease altogether from loading your estate with an ever-growing burden of debt. For goodness' sake leave these works alone. If you continue them you will simply beggar yourself.

TYR. (*uneasily*). I do not see that at all. The work will be very remunerative. It will double the value of the estate.

LORD S. Oh, Carden, listen to me. I know well the nature of such works as you are carrying on. I have tried them myself—on a far smaller scale, of course. They never repay their expenditure.

TYR. That is a mere assertion unsupported by argument. On the other hand, I have excellent reasons why I should believe that what I am about to undertake must have the best results. Look at the rich pasture now in the heather field. And am I to suppose that I shall not have the same in the valley when it is reclaimed? Until you can prove logically that I am mistaken, I must continue those works, which I clearly see are so profitable. Am I not right, Barry?

USS. I have said I shall never again discourage you, Carden.

LORD S. Ussher, upon my word I thought you knew better. But I suppose it is useless remonstrating on these experiments, which amount with him to absolute mania.

MRS GRACE TYRRELL *enters at back.*

GR. (*after bowing to* USSHER). Oh, Lord Shrule, we have been waiting for you in the garden. Won't you

41

come ?   I want to show you my little greenhouse.   The plants you gave me are doing so well in it.

LORD. S. I am delighted to hear you say so, Mrs Tyrrell.   Let us go and see them.   But I hope you will not make me walk much, as I have barely recovered from that last attack of gout, and can only get about as yet quietly on my pony.   Let me see, I left my hat in the hall.

GR. We can go through there, just as well.

[*Exeunt* LORD SHRULE *and* MRS GRACE TYRRELL
by door at right.

TYR. It is really too bad that I should be molested thus perpetually with unsolicited advice.   All my acquaintances seem to consider it incumbent upon them to interfere in and direct my affairs just like their own. One would think I had no right to do anything.   That old fellow, you know, means well ; but it is very annoying to be taken to task by a person who has really no right to meddle.   Ha !—it is too absurd indeed that I should have to defend what I have a perfect right to do.

MIL. I know it must be very trying, Carden.

TYR. I should think so, indeed.   And I am not going to stand it any longer.   I will live my life as I want, and will take dictation from nobody.

USS. But you must expect to be criticised, Carden. That is the penalty, you know, for attempting to do anything.

TYR. Oh, I don't mind any amount of outside criticism —nor even the strictures of friends like Lord Shrule, as long as their remarks are not to my face.   No, it is other criticism—nearer that leaves a sting.

42

MIL. Well, Carden, I am sure Barry and I are not in the habit of finding fault with you. At least we never mean to.

Uss. Of that, at all events, I am certain.

TYR. No—not you two, kindest and best. It is even nearer home—this criticism and opposition—this hearing perpetually amidst the strain of labour, bitter and disheartening words. That is what is so unbearable.

MIL. Be patient with her, Carden. Grace cannot as yet understand. This is a period of trial. One day you will see her loyally helping and inspiring you.

TYR. (*impatiently*). Inspiring me! I wish, Miles, you would not use a sublime word in a vulgar sense. When you have more experience you will find that instead of inspiring they more often prevent us from doing anything.

MIL. Oh, Carden—how unlike you! That is more the style of the cynic philosopher, there—Barry. See how he is smiling. I am sure he regrets he missed saying such a thing himself instead.

Uss. Well, really, Miles—

TYR. (*laughing*). Oh, you dear Miles. You were always the most wonderful body in the world for dispelling bitterness and gloom with that beautiful light you seem to carry about you! (*Hopefully*) Well, two friends such as you ought to compensate me for what I have to bear from others. Bah, I will not mind them. I will be merry while I work; and my work will be incessant, leaving no time for brooding over unpleasant things. And both of you will always be present with me, if difficulties should arise. Yes, with you I know I cannot suffer defeat from the rest.

43

Enter at back MRS GRACE TYRRELL, DOCTOR DOWLING, *a thick-set man of about forty, dressed in a tweed suit, and* DOCTOR ROCHE, *an elderly, lean and somewhat prim man, wearing spectacles and black clothes. Looking a little ill at ease, the* DOCTORS *exchange salutations with* TYRRELL, MILES, USSHER, *and* KIT.

KIT. Mother!

GR. Yes, my dear?

KIT. Who is that with Doctor Roche?

GR. Doctor Dowling.

KIT. Is he coming to see me too?

GR. Just to look at you, Kit. That's all.

KIT. But I have nothing the matter with me, mother.

GR. Never mind—neither will hurt you—only save you from possible peril—oh, my own sweet boy. (*She kisses him.*)

TYR. (*to* GRACE). You cannot think there was cause for summoning these two physicians.

GR. (*vaguely*). Cause?—well—I was a little anxious on the child's account, and thought it best they should consult about him. But I expected to find you alone. (*She glances at* USSHER).

USS. (*taking the hint*). Carden, I must go. I hope there is nothing really the matter with Kit. He doesn't look as if there was.

KIT. Oh, Barry, don't go. You know you promised—

USS. Hush, Kit.

TYR. Yes, stay where you are, Barry. There is no reason for making such a mystery of this business. Besides, I must soon go out to the inspector, and we can walk together. (*To* GRACE) By the way, what has become of the Shrules?

GR. (*uneasily*). Oh, Lord Shrule had to return home suddenly about some matter of importance.   They both desired me to say "good-bye" to you.

TYR. So much the better.—Well, doctors, I certainly cannot understand the necessity of this consultation. The boy seems to me perfectly well.

GR. No, I assure you, Doctor Dowling, he is not so. He is often ill from eating all sorts of unwholesome sweets.   How do you find him looking to-day, Doctor Roche ?

Roc. He appears healthier, on the whole, I think, Mrs Tyrrell.   (*To* KIT) Come here, and let me look well at you, my little man.   There, put out your tongue.

KIT. Ah, I suppose, Barry, I must now expect the worst.

Uss. Never fear, Kit.   They don't look as if they meant to do much to you.

GR. (*suspiciously*). I am afraid, Mr Ussher, you spoil him as much as his father, and I shall get no good of him while you are here.   You and Miles ought to take a walk.   It would be so nice on this fine day, wouldn't it ? But won't you return to dinner ?   Do return to dinner, Mr Ussher.

Uss. No, thank you, Mrs Tyrrell, I regret I cannot.   I shall be going now in a minute with Carden.   Kit must not expect any countenance from me.

KIT. But I thought you said you would not let Doctor Roche—

Uss. Now, Kit, you must do as you are told.   Have I not said you needn't fear ?

> [*The* DOCTORS *look at* KIT, *feel his pulse,*
> *talk together,* &c.

Uss. (*aside to* Miles). Your sister-in-law seems particularly anxious to get rid of us.

Mil. (*aside to* Ussher, *with an enquiring look*). Do you really think so?   I wonder why?

Uss. (*aside to* Miles). I am not certain yet.

Tyr. How needless this consultation is, to be sure. There is nothing the matter with the boy.

Gr. You do well to say so—you, who are the chief cause of his illness.

Tyr. I, the cause?

Gr. Of course you are.   He is sick at night after those long days when you keep him out fasting on the mountain, and then feed him with sweets at dinner afterwards.   This must all cease.

Kit. Oh, mother, do not prevent me from going to the heather field.   I don't want these sweets—I was only sick once.

Gr. Can you not see, Kit, that I am only acting for your good?   (*Sadly*) It is I who fight for his interests, and he leaves me for his father.

Tyr. Only sick once, and all this fuss for that!   Never mind, Kit, you shall not be prevented.   I will take care in future that you get plenty to eat and at proper times. So there will be no danger of sickness again.

Kit. Then you will not let anyone prevent me from going with you, father?

Tyr. Ah, you see, Kit, I never could get on without *you* in the heather field.   We should feel so lonely—both of us, shouldn't we?

[Grace *looks significantly at the* Doctors, *who now begin to observe* Tyrrell *closely.*

Kit. Yes, father, dear.

46

Uss. (*aside to* MILES). The doctors seem strangely in-attentive now to Kit and his ailments.

MIL. (*aside to* USSHER, *with a puzzled expression*). So it seems.   What do you think they mean?

Uss. (*aside to* MILES). Wait.   I have an uncomfortable suspicion.   It is well we stayed here.

GR. Alas, the child's health must be sacrificed like everything else, I suppose.

TYR. How sacrificed?

GR. Oh, to add zest to your infatuation for that mountain.

TYR. Nothing of the kind.   If I had known he had ever been ill, I would have taken every precaution, in spite of my infatuation as you choose to call the interest I take in my work.

Dow. Is that your land work, Mr Tyrrell?

TYR. Yes.

Dow. You are an extensive reclaimer of waste land?

TYR. Yes; I fancy there are few in Ireland more extensive.

Roc. You are certainly most enterprising.

TYR. Ay—it is a grand work.

Dow. And you believe in the possibility of its paying?

TYR. Of course.   Wait till you see the profits I shall make.   With these I shall extend my works; and with the further profits I shall embark on such a scale of business as in time will enable me to start a company for buying up and reclaiming or reafforesting every inch of waste land in Ireland.

Uss. That is truly a gigantic scheme, Carden.   Look here, I must really be going; and your inspector, too, must be waiting for you.   Let us be off.   Come along.

TYR. Oh, wait a moment, Barry. I want to explain.
I will go with you directly. (*To the* DOCTORS) With
the far-reaching usefulness of my projects I must become
a real benefactor to the country, and in a time, too, when
so many quack remedies in the way of legislation are being
offered to the public.

ROC. True, true. How very interesting.

DOW. Upon my word, most interesting.

TYR. Oh, the work is a glorious one. There is something creative about it—this changing the face of a whole
country! None of the humdrum, barn-door work of
ordinary farming, with its sordid accompaniment of the
cattle fair! When from the ideal world of my books
those people forced me to such a business, I was bound
to find the extreme of its idealisation.

DOW. (*aside to* DOCTOR ROCHE). What the dickens
does he mean by that?

ROC. You mean you have idealised farming, Mr
Tyrrell?

TYR. Of course, what else? Do you think I could go
on doing the dull drudgery they forced upon me? No—
I considered how I could elevate it. I pondered and
pondered and never rested, until at last there came to me
the master-thought of the heather-field.

ROC. (*slowly nodding assent*). Oh,—indeed. Dear
me.

TYR. (*with evident pleasure at the surprise he is creat-
ing*). Yes; was it not a discovery? And what contentment it brought after the previous life-drudgery. I felt
like returning to my youth's ideals in that free mountain
air. Oh! there is magic in those mountain breezes!

DOW. All I know, sir, is, that the Faculty consider sea

air blowing over a mountain bog to be the finest remedy in the world for bile or dyspepsia. (*He looks around him facetiously.*)

Tyr. (*with an expression of disgust*). So that is the only thought suggested to you by the ethereal mountain breeze ! There are some people who can never recognize a beautiful meaning in anything.

Dow. Maybe so, Mr Tyrrell. (*As if struck with an idea*) Do you find any meaning yourself, though, in this mountain air ?

Tyr. (*disdainfully*). Do I ? Why, of course I do. I find in it a medium between the beauty of the past and myself.

Dow. Indeed.

Tyr. Yes ; nature's ethereal phonograph, as it might be, treasuring for my delight past ecstasies of sound. I hear in its waves those voices floating back to me from—

Uss. (*with alarm, aside to* Miles). You must take your brother away at once.

Dow. What is that you are saying, Mr Tyrrell ?

Roc. Voices—you don't mean to say you hear voices ?

Tyr. I do mean to say it.

Dow. Whose voices do you hear ?

Tyr. Choristers singing of youth in an eternal sunrise !

Roc. But you must know that this is all imagination.

Tyr. (*irritably*). Imagination — always imagination. How wearisome that word sounds to me. I tell you there is no such thing as imagination.

Dow. That is a bold statement, sir.

Tyr. No—you either perceive or you don't perceive. Therefore it vexes me, when I perceive anything, to be told that it is only imagination.

D   49

Gr. Wouldn't it be more accurate, then, to call it hallucination?

Tyr. (*hastily to her*). That's always how you enter into the spirit of my ideas.

Dow. You can hardly expect her to agree with them.

Tyr. (*resignedly*). No—I suppose there must always be distortion of my meaning.

Dow. Then would you mind explaining your meaning?

Roc. You told us you hear voices?

Tyr. Yes, of course.

Roc. Do you ever remember anything they say?

Tyr. (*thinking*). Yes.

Dow. Well, would you let us know?

Tyr. They keep telling me I am not what I am.

Roc. How very strange!

Dow. Humph! do they say anything else, sir?

Tyr. They often call me back to my real life.

Roc. What do you mean by your real life?

Tyr. That life before I wandered into this dream.

Dow. And so you think you are only dreaming now?

Tyr. How can you tell that *you* also are not now in a dream?

Uss. Answer that, if you are able, doctor.

Dow. A man ought to know very well whether he is asleep or awake.

Tyr. That is just it; and I know I am in a dream.

Uss. (*impatiently*). Really, Carden, I don't see what you gain by discussing your ideas with people who can neither understand nor sympathize with them. Come, come away. I cannot wait any longer.

Tyr. (*rather dejected*). Yes, Barry, I suppose you are

right. It was stupid of me. Let us go out. Good evening, doctors.

Uss. (*to* TYRRELL). You walk on with Miles and Kit. I just remember I have something to consult Doctor Roche about.

MIL. Come, Carden.

[*Exeunt at back* CARDEN, MILES, *and* KIT TYRRELL.

Uss. (*very gravely*). Doctor Dowling and Doctor Roche, you were sent for by Mrs Tyrrell to-day to consult on a matter altogether different from the health of the little boy.

GR. (*defiantly*). Well, then, and if they were!

Uss. Your husband fortunately suspects nothing; and I have warned Miles against saying anything to enlighten him.

GR. If you consider me in your power, you are greatly mistaken.

Uss. (*austerely*). I consider nothing of the sort, Mrs Tyrrell. You have strangely misunderstood me.

GR. I don't know. Anyhow, I have nothing to fear from you. The opinions of Doctor Dowling and Doctor Roche will ensure the success of the measures I have decided upon for the security of the child's interests and mine.

Uss. You seem very sure as to the conclusions these gentlemen are to arrive at.

GR. Well, they know all about my poor husband's reckless expenditure, his inability to act like other people, his futile disputes with the tenantry, and to-day they have seen how he has conducted himself, and have heard him speak. I hardly think they can have any doubt as to the condition of his mind. What do you say, Doctor Dowling and Doctor Roche?

Dow. I am of opinion, ma'am, it is a case of dementia —but curable with proper treatment.

Uss. Indeed.   And what are your reasons for considering it dementia?

Dow. The general tenor, Mr Ussher, of the patient's behaviour; his reckless expenditure of his means, as Mrs Tyrrell says; his queer deranged enthusiasm; and, above all, his talk about hearing voices. There is no more common sign of insanity than for persons to believe that they hear voices.

Roc. Quite so.   That is by far the most serious symptom in the case.

Uss. But surely you must see that a highly-gifted man like Carden Tyrrell is not to be judged by your everyday rules. These voices you speak of he heard long ago in happier days. They are only memories made vivid by the force of imagination. Why, he told you as much. Did he not?

Dow. That was not the impression conveyed to me.

Uss. Doctor Roche, you cannot agree with this, I am sure.

Roc. Well, really, Mr Ussher, I fear I must—that is to say, with certain reservations. Our responsibility in certifying to madness is no doubt grave; but then, on the other hand, we would incur a graver responsibility if, by our indulgence, the patient afterwards were to harm himself or anyone else.

Gr. If he is not restrained he will surely bring the child and me to irreparable ruin. You see he has almost done so already. Oh, think of that, Doctor Roche. You know he is not fit to have the control of anything.

Roc. I know there might be some doubt as to the

question of madness, if we had nothing more to go upon than these extravagant land improvements of his.

Uss. (*eagerly*). Yes.

Roc. But then I am confronted by this unpleasant symptom of his hearing voices that have no existence—a most common sign, as you say rightly, Dowling, of insanity.

Uss. Did not Joan of Arc declare she heard voices calling on her to accomplish a work which proved to be one of the most wonderful and practical in history? Was not Socrates firmly convinced that he was in the habit of receiving admonitions from his dæmon? I might quote you several other instances of celebrated personages whose imaginations led them to believe they heard voices. Yet no one has ever thought of calling them insane. Come now, Doctor Roche, a man of your experience and culture must admit the truth of what I say.

Roc. Ah, Mr Ussher, I fear all forms of madness might be explained away by your arguments.

Gr. Of course, Doctor Roche. Pray don't listen to him.

Roc. But, at the same time, Mrs Tyrrell, I am bound to admit that madness partakes more of an infirmity whereby the natural sequence of ideas is disconnected.

Uss. Quite so, quite so. If you talk with a lunatic you find that you can never keep him to any consecutive line of thought. He is perpetually off here, off there, on some new and irrelevant tangent. You can never obtain a direct answer to a question. His mental process resembles a chain, at intervals unlinked. These are the real symptoms of that pitiful and uninteresting malady. Are they not?

53

Roc. Yes, Mr Ussher, on the whole you are fairly right.

Uss. Very well then, are any such symptoms discoverable in Carden Tyrrell?   Who is more clearly consecutive in his ideas than he?   Discuss any question with him—politics or books—what you will—I am bound he acquits himself ably.

Gr. And land improvement too, Mr Ussher, you forget that.

Dow. There you just have it, ma'am.

Uss. His reasons for making these improvements are quite consecutive and rational. (Doctor Dowling *and* Grace *laugh*.)   Oh, but I assure you they are so.   His work may or may not be practical.   Who knows?   Personally I agree with you in thinking it is not.   Still, that is no plea for trying to deprive him of his liberty and rights.   If it were, I fear that many, and those too in responsible positions, might have their freedom of action endangered.   It is only common-place and unimaginative people who consider the poetic and original temperament to be a mark of madness.

Roc. There is a great deal in what you say, Mr Ussher. I—

Gr. (*alarmed*). Doctor Roche, you cannot be serious? You are not giving in to such arguments?

Roc. (*apologetically*). No—no, Mrs Tyrrell.   I merely admit their truth in a general way.   That is all.

Uss. You are far too clever a man, Doctor, not to see their truth.   Then again, think of the gravity and danger of what you propose doing.   You know, of course, gentlemen, that you will be asked to confirm on oath before a Commission of Lunacy the opinion you now so rashly form of my friend.

Dow. I am quite prepared, Sir, to swear before any Commission.

Uss. That may be, Doctor Dowling. However, Doctor Roche, the matter doubtless appears in another light to you. You may be quite certain that when Carden Tyrrell is forewarned, he will be particularly careful not to compromise himself at his private examination by the Commission, who will then, of course, ridicule the idea of preventing him from managing his estate. The defeated parties afterwards will be open to an action by their victim for damages, of which action the law costs, whether he succeeds or not, are sure to be considerable on all sides. When this conspiracy—

Gr. Mr Ussher, you forget yourself. How dare you—?

Uss. Yes, Mrs Tyrrell, it is an unpleasant word, but excusable in my resentment of this cruel injustice to my old and best friend. You may be sure, too, it is the word the world will use. Why did the Shrules leave here so suddenly to-day?

Gr. (*haughtily*). You have already heard the reason.

Uss. I am bound to accept it. But I cannot help thinking that Lord Shrule invented his excuse.

Gr. I think we have heard quite enough from you, Mr Ussher. You are not likely to intimidate us by your threats. (*To the* Doctors) Isn't that so?

Dow. Oh, I am prepared to stand by my opinion, ma'am.

Gr. And you, Doctor Roche—?

Roc. (*nervously*). Well, you see, Mrs Tyrrell, I never held so decided an opinion of the case as my friend Doctor Dowling. I think—for the present—that is to say—perhaps—

55

Gr. For the present? Surely you must know that if we do not act at once we shall be too late to prevent the raising of this ruinous loan.

Roc. Ah, yes, yes, but I am afraid I cannot make up my mind about the patient as yet. I could not undertake to swear on oath that he is now insane.

Gr. It is quite clear that you are intimidated, Doctor Roche.

Roc. (*indignantly*). I allow no one to intimidate me, Mrs Tyrrell.

Gr. And you will leave the child and me to be ruined?

Roc. What can I do? Have I not told you my difficulties?

Gr. Oh, Doctor Roche, we are in your hands. Our fate lies upon your decision. I implore of you not to fail us.

Roc. (*very confused*). You must excuse me, Mrs Tyrrell; but on consideration I would not venture to grant your request. I have an appointment just now. Pray excuse me. Good afternoon, Mrs Tyrrell. Good afternoon, good afternoon.   [*Exit, bowing to all, at back.*

Dow. Well, I suppose after this I am not much use here, so I may as well also be on my way. I am sorry, ma'am, the Doctor was persuaded to change his mind; but he is a nervous, timid man. To me the case seems a pretty clear one. However, perhaps it is better to do nothing just at present.

                    [*He bows, and exit by door at back.*

Gr. (*to* Ussher, *with suppressed anger.*) I suppose you are prepared to bear the responsibility you have incurred.

Uss. Yes—I am prepared to bear it. But did you

fully consider the responsibility you were so eager to take upon yourself, Mrs Tyrrell?   I can only hope that you had not considered the question.

GR. I do not understand you.

USS. I am sorry for it.   Is it then so light a matter to imprison a man,—and above all such a man as your husband?   It would practically mean his death.   To take him away from all that he loves,—his free life on the mountains, his intimate delight in nature, his interests and occupations, without which life would become for him meaningless—can you not understand the cruelty of this?

GR. I have no wish to be cruel.   I must only protect myself.

USS. Yes — but it seems to me in attempting this protection you are very inexorable — very cruel.   And the worst of it is, you appear not to realise the cruelty which you are so ready to inflict.   Have you forgotten that he is your husband, that he once loved you very dearly?   Have you forgotten everything except yourself?

GR. I have not forgotten my child—

USS. You are, of course, bound to think of him, but not, I am sure, to the detriment of your husband.   Carden has his rights as well as Kit.   Is the father to be wholly sacrificed for the child?   (*Pause.*)   But, Mrs Tyrrell, were you only thinking of your child?

GR. What do you mean?

USS. Was there not another reason besides the child which caused you to be so resolute?   That personal dislike—   Remember you and Carden have not been living very amicably for some time.

Gr. Oh—you consider that ill-feeling has actuated me in this matter?

Uss. I don't say so—I only suggest the probability. Are you sure that it is not so?

Gr. (*indignantly*). What a base insinuation. No—I am sure it is not so—of course it is not so. I may no longer care for my husband. Perhaps I never cared much for him. But I know that now I am only thinking of my child. It was for little Kit's sake that I wished—

Uss. Yes—to imprison his father in a madhouse.

Gr. I was willing to accept the responsibility. Are you still willing to accept yours? It is a heavy one. There was a chance of saving our fortune; and you have wrecked it. What will you now do to save the child and me from this madman who is devouring our substance?

Uss. Hush—hush. For heaven's sake do not talk in this manner.

Gr. Oh, why did you do me this cruel wrong to-day?

Uss. I only prevented your doing a cruel wrong.

Gr. You have done us all a cruel wrong.

Uss. No—I feel I have done you all a good deed to-day.

Gr. (*scornfully*). A good deed truly—a deed giving power to carry out those projects which are our ruin!

Uss. Who can tell but that his projects may succeed? Be patient. Be gentle with him. I believe you might win him yet by gentleness from very great extravagance. Try.

Gr. (*gloomily*). Too late.

Uss. Why too late?

58

GR. It was too late from the moment his thoughts first turned to the heather field.

USS. (*starts and looks at her for a moment with vague alarm.   Then says very gently*) There is no reason why he should ever learn the part you have played against him to-day.   Henceforth you will be different to him, will you not?

GR. (*gazing steadfastly before her*). Too late—

USS. Ah—well—   [*Exit quietly at back.*

[*Pause.   There is a noise as of some one approaching.   GRACE looks out at back, then recedes to door at right.   CARDEN TYRRELL enters hurriedly, carrying a sheet of the ordnance map, which he lays upon the writing-table at left and studies, unaware of his wife's presence.   She watches him with an expression of gathering anger, then exit sobbing by door at right.   He starts and turns to see her just disappear, then sighing he shrugs his shoulders, and resumes his eager study of the map.*

(*End of Act II.*)

ACT III

SCENE :—The same as last, only that the place, by the absence of all drawing-room ornaments, has assumed once more its aspect of a library. A fire of fresh ashwood in the large fire-place burns cheerfully, while sunlight streams in through the window-doors at back. A sheet of the ordnance map lies on writing table. Several months have passed ; and it is now Spring.

KIT TYRRELL runs in by door at right carrying a child's kite, which he examines as he kneels down in front of the fire. Measuring out the string at arm's length, he appears dissatisfied. Then, as if suddenly remembering, he runs over to the book-case at back, and climbing up on its ledge he takes from behind the books on an upper row a mass of cord. He returns, and disentangling it ties its end to the cord attached to the kite, which he then carries to the window-doors at back. These he opens, and stands in a flood of sunlight. Outside is heard the singing of birds.

CARDEN TYRRELL, somewhat aged and careworn, enters by door at right.

TYR. (*half to himself as he watches* KIT). Oh, memories—

KIT. (*after a short pause, perceiving* TYRRELL *and running to him*). Father.

TYR. The little birds are singing in the sunlight to my little bird. Where are you going, Kit?

KIT. I am going to fly the kite. Oh, come out, father, with me to the heather field. There is sure to be a splendid breeze there to-day.

TYR. (*sadly*). Ah, the heather field. No, Kit, I cannot.

KIT. You have not been there for such a long time. Why can't you come?

60

TYR. I can't; it is unbearable to be always followed and watched—and in that place above all others.

KIT. But, father, why don't you tell those policemen to go away?

TYR. I have done so over and over again. They will not go.

KIT. But why must they watch you, father, dear?

TYR. (*looks at* KIT *for a moment, then in an unsteady voice as he turns away*). Do not ask me, boy. You would not understand.

KIT. (*catching* TYRRELL *by the arm*). Really? Yet Barry says that I understand so many things better than if I were a man.

TYR. (*thoughtfully*). He is right. Only those who become as you are, can know the rarest joys of life.

KIT. Then why do you think, father, I would not understand the reason they are watching you.

TYR. Because—because it would appear—well, something incredible to you. There, do not ask, boy. (*He flings himself moodily into the chair on the outside of the writing table. A short pause.*)

KIT. (*coming near*). Father, dear, you are not angry with me?

TYR. No, Kit. Only a bit worried by things in general.

KIT. I am sorry if I have ever worried you. I will try not to do it again. I love you. Oh, you don't know how I love you, father.

TYR. (*throwing his arms around* KIT). My darling, you have never worried me. I could not live without you.

KIT. (*hiding his face on* TYRRELL's *neck*). Oh, father, father!

TYR. Yes, Kit, you are the little elf that calls up for

61

me the magic of the heather field. Henceforth we must never be divided—you and I. `

KIT. Never, oh never, father dear. You don't know how lonely I feel away from you. I have not been to the heather field for ever so long. It seemed such a sad place when you were not there.

TYR. Even in spite of its wild flowers, Kit? It is time for them now to be coming out again.

KIT. Yes, the heather field will be beginning to look lovely now.

TYR. How I wish I were free to walk among its flowers on this soft spring day.

KIT. Poor father!—but would you like me to fetch you some of them. Shall I go?

TYR. Yes, do, Kit. I should like some flowers from the heather field.

BARRY USSHER *enters at back.*

KIT. Oh, there's Barry.

TYR. What—Barry! It is an event when I see anyone now.

USS. As if it were not your own doing.

TYR. (*somewhat ruffled*). You may say what you like for all I care.

USS. (*shrugging his shoulders*). Heigh-ho! Well, Kit, are you glad the winter is over?

KIT. Oh, yes, how horrid and dark it was.

USS. I wonder how you ever managed to exist through it. And you never got the pony, after all?

KIT. No—you see when father promised me one he thought he could afford it. But now he cannot, until he lets the heather field. I must wait a while longer. Is not that so, father?

Tyr. Yes, Kit, we must wait.

Kit. You know, Barry, I could not think of worrying him any more about the pony.

Uss. You good little son, there is no need to wait any longer. I have just brought you such a nice pony.

Tyr. What is this, Barry? what is this?

Kit. Oh, where is he, Barry?

Uss. Out in the yard waiting for you—bridle, saddle and all.

Kit. Oh, thank you, Barry. Father, is he not nice and kind?

Tyr. (*looking at* Ussher). Yes, always the kind friend —always the same.

Kit. Father, I shall ride the pony off to the heather-field at once, and get you those flowers.   [*Exit at back.*

Uss. How happy the little fellow is.

Tyr. You have indeed made him so by your kindness, Barry.

Uss. Bah—a selfish kindness at most. I tell you, I have not felt for a long time such real happiness as just now when I saw myself looked at like some good spirit by that little face.

Tyr. And to think that you who are so lucky, to whom most things come so easily, should say this! Why, even I, with all my troubles, could hardly speak more despondingly. What would you do if you were imprisoned as I am here since those evictions?

Uss. Your health will be ruined by your obstinacy.

Tyr. What can I do? The police have orders never to lose sight of me if I go out. They say I should be shot at otherwise.

Uss. Ha!

TYR. And you know I never could bear to be followed by a guard. It makes me feel like a criminal. I would much rather stay indoors.

Uss. (*after thinking for a moment*). Look here, Carden, you ought to leave this place for a while. We will go together. We will travel.

TYR. Impossible, the drainage of the valley could never go on in my absence.

Uss. Why not? You haven't been near it for ever so long.

TYR. Oh, that doesn't matter in the least. I can direct it just as well from this room. There on the writing table is my map with all the drains marked upon it. The superintendent comes to me at stated intervals, reports the progress of each man's work, and takes the fresh orders which I give him from the map. I assure you it gives me greater pleasure to conduct operations in this way scientifically, than if I were to go on the ground. One can imagine oneself in such a situation, like Moltke fighting battles from his study.

Uss. (*gives a quick look at* TYRRELL. *Then after a short pause*—) Well, if you won't leave here, at all events try and settle with those peasants, so that you may dispense with police and be able to go about again.

TYR. Settle? How could I settle with them? The only settlement they would hear of I could never grant. Oh no—a nice ending, indeed, that would be to our battle!

Uss. Is there no compromise you will come to?

TYR. I will reinstate the evicted, if they pay in full their rents and the costs I have incurred on their account.

Uss. Oh, that is no compromise at all.

TYR. Well, it is as much as I can agree to. I told these people when they struck, that I could not afford to give abatements on rents which had already been reduced so much by the Land Commission, and I can less afford to give any now with pressing mortgagees who have not been paid for so long.

Uss. But would it not be better to get some rent for that land instead of leaving it idle?   Others, you know, will not dare to take it from you.

Tyr. I cannot help that.   I must work it myself.

Uss. Meanwhile how are you going to pay the mortgagees their interest?

Tyr. Oh, there is the great difficulty.   The chief mortgagee is most pressing, and threatens to foreclose immediately.   I have implored of him again and again to wait until I can let the heather field, but in vain.   Miles, whom I expect home this evening, was to have made a final appeal to him in Dublin last night.   I can only hope for a favourable result.

Uss. I think you had better come to terms with those tenants, Carden.

Tyr. I shall never give in to them.   I shall never voluntarily reduce the value of my property.   Besides, if the worst should come, I have always the great resource.

Uss. What is that?

Tyr. The heather field!

Uss. Carden, take care.   It is a dangerous thing— trusting to only one resource.

Tyr. (*a little irritated*). What do you mean?   Are you too going to join the enemy?

Uss. (*uneasily*). No, no, Carden, you do not understand me; but——

Tyr. But what?

Uss. Oh, I should so like to see you on good terms

E   65

with your people again. I am sure the remembrance of all that friendship with them in the past must make this quarrel unbearable to you.

TYR. Yes, indeed that is true.

USS. And this continual watch upon your movements too must be dreadful.

TYR. Dreadful, it is gradually wearing me out. I know I cannot stand it much longer. And most of the long dreary winter I had no one about me whom I could confide in or consult; for Miles has been away at College as you know.

USS. Yes, carrying everything before him. I see he has won a scholarship. He is sure of his gold medal now.

TYR. Miles is of the stuff to succeed. I am so fond of Miles. He was always such good company.

USS. Of course, a most charming boy. I am glad he is to be at home to-day.

TYR. Indeed his companionship will make a great difference to me, now that I can never get about.

USS. (*anxiously*). Oh, but Carden, you cannot continue in this way. You have always been used to so free a life in the open air. I say this imprisonment will kill you. Already I see a very marked change in your appearance.

TYR. (*doggedly*). I cannot help it. My past demands that I must suffer.

    [*With a sigh, he passes to right of doors at back, where he looks out in a reverie.*

USS. (*watching him*). For heaven's sake, Carden, do not be so fatally unreasonable.

TYR. (*after a pause, still looking in the same direction*). No—I am not so; you think those remedies you suggest would avail to relieve me—but they would not.

Uss. Why not?

Tyr. You ask—you who are such a philosopher? Can you not understand that the only remedy for me must be something that has no relation whatever with those circumstances that may affect me ill or otherwise?

Uss. You mean that improvement of circumstances has little to do with bringing contentment.

Tyr. I mean that the only remedy must be something which would make me forgetful that I am myself. (*Mysteriously*) Barry, would you believe it, often in moments of darkest anxiety I am arrested by the sight of some flower or leaf or some tiny nook in the garden out there. And oh—I become then at once so peaceful that I care not what may happen to me. I think it is only when we turn to them in our misery that we can really see the exquisite beauty of these things.

Uss. Ah, Carden, nature is a marvellous sedative. How infinite her ingenuousness amidst all our pains and fears.

Tyr. Yes—and just this moment when I looked upon the ocean there and the land awakening with such freshness from its winter sleep, I felt something that no improvement of circumstances could bring. (*Then with a strange enthusiasm*) Oh, to feel that despite all suffering one has the firmament, the earth, the sea! What more can one really require from the world?

Uss. Ay—true enough. "For all things were made from these," to quote the great mediæval philosopher. Nevertheless I think I might bring you another and very real sort of relief from this present trouble, if you would but allow me.

Tyr. And what if you might? It would only be succeeded by some further trouble. That is the only sort of relief you could ever bring. Ah, there is a trouble past all your remedies.

Uss. Alas, I fear there are many. How could I pretend otherwise ? But will you tell me this particular one ?

Tyr. I wonder will you understand.

Uss. Why not, Carden ?

Tyr. Well then, have you ever seen on earth something beautiful beyond earth—that great beauty which appears in divers ways ? And then have you known what it is to go back to the world again ?

Uss. (*sadly*). I know, I know—the pain of loss.

Tyr. Is it not misery ? But you have seen the great beauty have you not ? Oh, that immortal beauty—so far away—always so far away.

Uss. Yes—yes, our ideal of beauty that for ever haunts and eludes us through life. (*With a movement of resignation*) But let us not speak of it any more.

Tyr. Why, Barry ?

Uss. Because, as you say, it makes one so miserable in the world, and it is such a hopeless phantom after all.

Tyr. How can you say so ? You who know that it is alone the reality in the world.

Uss. (*cautiously*). Hush, Carden, I do not know.

Tyr. (*laughing bitterly*). There—just like you, Barry, careful never to let yourself go.

Uss. No—no, Carden, but you brood too much on these thoughts. You are overworked—you ought really to come away from here. Do let us travel somewhere together for a change.

Tyr. Ah, not now—at some future time, perhaps— but not now. My difficulties are gathering before me. I must stand and hew them from my path.

GRACE TYRRELL *enters hurriedly and excitedly by door at right.*

GR. (*pauses when she sees* USSHER, *then to* TYRRELL). Oh, but I suppose as you have no secrets from him——

TYR. (*starting*). Well, what is the matter?

GR. (*holding out a paper*). A dreadful - looking man has just handed me this.

TYR. Let me see (*takes paper*). Ah——

GR. I have so often asked you for money to pay this person.

TYR. I am very sorry. I had nothing to give you.

GR. Alas, you always had plenty to squander on that mountain.

TYR. That was Government money, and it could not honestly be expended except on the object for which it was advanced.

GR. I am afraid I must have some of it now. I cannot be left in this condition.

TYR. Indeed you shall not have one penny of it.

GR. What—you mean to leave me under the stigma of such an insult?

TYR. (*impatiently*). There is no particular urgency. I will see if I can possibly meet this writ by some money of my own. (*With a painful distracted look*) Oh this worry—this worry. [*Exit by door at right.*

GR. Well, Mr Ussher, I hope you are satisfied now. We are ruined; and my husband is becoming stranger in his behaviour every day. But for you, he might have been cured by this, and the estate in a very different condition.

USS. I have nothing, Mrs Tyrrell, to reproach myself with. I did all for the best.

GR. Yes, of course. That is the only satisfaction one

ever receives for injuries done through gratuitous inter-
ference.

Uss. Nothing has since happened to convict me of
having acted wrongly.   I have done you no injury.

GR. No injury?   Well!

Uss. You cannot lay to my account this quarrel
with the tenants which is the cause of your present
difficulties.   Goodness knows I have done my best to
mend it.

GR. (*impatiently*). Oh, that is only a temporary difficulty.   But the estate will be ruined for ever by the great
debt from which we should have saved it, if you had not
interfered.   (*Pause.*)   Yes—I see now how it all will be.
The child and I will be driven out, ruined, to battle with
the world.

Uss. Oh, don't think of such a thing, Mrs Tyrrell.   It
can never come to that.

GR. (*sadly*). Ah, yes.   You destroyed my last chance
of saving our home.   I might have kept it lovingly for
Kit until he grew to be a man ; but now I see it must go
from us.   I shall have to bid everything farewell—the
familiar rooms—the garden where I found an occupation
for my life—even those common useless things about the
house I have been accustomed to look at for years.   Oh,
you don't know what it is—this parting from those everyday things of one's life.

Uss. Yes, yes—indeed I do—and from my heart I feel
for you.

GR. And yet you could have acted as you have.

Uss. I acted only in good faith.   Heaven knows that
is the truth.

GR. The injury remains still the same.

70

ACT III.   THE HEATHER FIELD

Uss. (*with strong emotion*). If it is I who have injured you, Mrs Tyrrell, you must allow me to make amends.

Gr. Alas, what amends are possible?

Uss. Who can tell?   I promise you, at least, you shall never, *never* bid farewell to your home.

Gr. (*in a trembling voice*). If only what you say might come true.

LADY SHRULE, LORD SHRULE, *and* CARDEN TYRRELL
enter by door at right.

LORD S. Carden, I believe your servant was actually going to say "not at home" to us, if I had not caught sight of you in the hall.   Ha, ha.

LADY S. What a shame, Mr Tyrrell, to try and prevent me from seeing Grace.   How do you do, Grace dear? (*Giving her hand apathetically to* USSHER) How do you do?

LORD S. (*shakes hands with* GRACE *and* USSHER). We should have been so disappointed.

TYR. I assure you, Lord Shrule, my attempt to escape is purely an imagination on your part.

LORD S. Oh, you sly fellow, you think I do not know. You are just like your father when people used to call— although he would never run away from me, I can tell you.

TYR. No more did I.   I was only surprised to see you; that was all.   When I heard the bell I thought it was Miles come from Dublin.   I am anxiously expecting him now at any moment.

LORD S. Ah, it will be a pleasure to see Miles again. We have all heard of his University triumphs.   How proud your poor father would have been.

71

TYR. Yes, and how delighted to share his satisfaction with you.

LORD S. Poor Marmaduke, we were such friends—at our very last interview he asked me to keep you and your brother always in mind after he was gone. So I have always felt somehow like a father towards you both, you know, and with a father's privilege occasionally have given advice.

GR. Yes, Lord Shrule, and how I wish your good advice occasionally had been followed.

LORD S. Ah, we cannot help that, Mrs Tyrrell. Nothing will ever teach the young save bitter experience.

GR. I am sure there has been enough bitter experience; but it seems to have taught nothing at all.

LORD S. Well, well, I hope it won't be so. Eh, Carden?

TYR. I do not see how my experience can teach me to act differently from my present way of acting. (*Aside to* USSHER) Miles ought to have arrived by this. Oh, I am nearly dead with anxiety to know the news he will bring.

USS. (*aside to* TYRRELL). I hope there will be good news.

LORD S. Never mind, Mrs Tyrrell. Carden will come by degrees to see his mistakes.

GR. I fear we are now in so bad a way that it does not much matter whether he sees them or not.

LADY S. No—really, Grace, you do not say so?

GR. Oh, Lilian, we are ruined.

LORD S. Come, come, I am sure it cannot be as bad as that.

Tyr. Goodness me, of course not, Lord Shrule. On the contrary, in the near future we shall make a fortune.

Gr. I say we are ruined, utterly, irretrievably.

Tyr. No—no——

Uss. What noise is that? (*Listens, then opens door at right.*) Why, Miles has arrived.

Tyr. Miles—oh!

Uss. There, Carden, for goodness sake be calm.

Enter MILES TYRRELL *by door at right.*

Mil. Carden. (*He grasps his brother by the hand, then greets all the rest.*)

Tyr. What news, Miles? Will he wait?

Mil. (*turning away dejectedly*). I did my best, Carden. There is no hope, I fear.

Gr. No hope? What is this new misfortune? Who won't wait?

Mil. The chief mortgagee.

Gr. Is he going to foreclose?

Mil. He says so.

Lord S. Ha—this is a most serious matter.

Tyr. But Miles, didn't you explain to him all about the heather field?

Mil. Yes.

Tyr. Didn't you assure him that it would soon bring in what would more than pay his interest?

Mil. Indeed I did, Carden.

Tyr. Well?

Mil. Well, that only seemed to make him impatient with me. But I used every argument I could think of, and pleaded with him for nearly an hour in his office, until at last he had to get rid of me almost brutally.

73

Tyr. (*with a look of humiliation and despair*). Oh ruin! ruin!

Uss. No, no, Carden—it is not yet that. We must see how we can help you through this difficulty.

Tyr. (*quietly*). With all your goodwill, Barry, what can you do now?

Uss. Who knows? Just keep quiet, and do not distress yourself. Leave it all to me.

Tyr. (*almost staggering*). Yes—such a severe blow—this. It has quite upset me. I am sure you will all excuse me. You, Barry, will see what you can do, won't you? Yes— (*He goes to door at right.*)

Uss. Yes, Carden, I hope all will come well.

Lord S. How much of the property does this mortgage cover?

Gr. Oh, pretty nearly all, I should think.

Tyr. (*suddenly turning*). All, do you say? No—not all. This vulture cannot touch the heather field! My hope—it is my only hope now, and it will save me in the end. Ha, ha! these wise ones! They did not think the barren mountain of those days worth naming in their deed. But now that mountain is a great green field worth more than all they can seize, (*with a strange intensity*) and it is mine—all mine!

[*Exit by door at right.*

Lord S. (*throwing up his hands*). Oh dear, oh dear, what infatuation!

Gr. Yes indeed, it has caused us all to be cast adrift in the world. Oh, what is to become of me—what is to become of me? (*She sobs in her handkerchief.*)

Lady S. Grace, you must not lose heart.

GR. Ah, the final misfortune has come.

LADY S. We shall try and help you, dear—there.

USS. Yes, we must lose no time now to see what can be done for Carden.

LADY S. You should indeed bestir yourself, Mr Ussher, and save him; for we have you to thank that he was left in a position to ruin himself.

USS. And have not you too, Lady Shrule, to thank yourself for the same thing?

LADY S. I? How so, pray?

USS. Why did you and Lord Shrule disappear so suddenly on that day the doctors were here? Your advocacy would doubtless have made them heedless of my objections—

LADY S. Ha—why indeed? You know, Shrule, I wanted you to——

LORD S. Well, well, I could not bear to act in such a way to the son of my old friend. But I suppose in my weakness I did wrong.

USS. No, Lord Shrule, you did right. You never could be suspected by anyone of doing otherwise.

LORD S. I hope not, Ussher! Still, I am inclined to think it might have been wiser then to have taken some definite step.

LADY S. I should think so. Just see what has happened since.

GR. Nothing less than the ruin of a helpless woman and her child.

LADY S. You have, indeed, incurred a nice responsibility, Mr Ussher.

GR. (*to* USSHER). What—what right had you to do my child and me this wrong?

75

Uss. I only prevented what I thought a grievous wrong from being done to my friend.

GR. It was no wrong—it was for his good—for all our good. In your heart you must know I was right.

Uss. I have often said, Mrs Tyrrell, I know nothing of the sort.

LADY S. Still, you must admit that his actions since more than justify Mrs Tyrrell in the course she adopted.

LORD S. Alas, I fear that is the case.

Uss. I admit he is very wilful and extravagant, but no more. I cannot discover any mental infirmity. His mind has a perfect grasp of ideas.

GR. Don't talk of ideas. I have heard enough about them since I was married to give me a horror of them for the rest of my life.

LADY S. They have certainly caused the wreck of this household.

LORD S. Oh, I hope not. We must not be too pessimistic.—Who can tell?—perhaps the heather field may turn out a success after all !

GR. (*with contempt*). The heather field.

LORD S. If it were to, there can be no doubt but that all would be saved. I wonder how it is going on. Have you been there lately, Mrs Tyrrell ?

GR. Of course not, Lord Shrule. The very thought of the place fills me with despair.

MIL. That is a pity, Grace—a great pity, when so much depends upon the success of the heather field.

GR. No good can ever come of that abominable work.

MIL. You must not speak such words ; no luck can come from such words.

76

GR. I cannot help it.

MIL. Oh, I know you have much to endure, but I cannot remain here and listen to such denunciation of what my brother holds nearest to his heart.

GR. I have only said the truth.

MIL. You cannot be certain. of this truth. It is not right to speak such words.   [*Exit by door at right.*

LADY S. My poor Grace.

GR. Oh, Lilian.

LADY S. These troubles are driving you to distraction. You had better leave this place for a while. Will you not come and stay with us?

LORD S. Oh yes, won't you stay with us, Mrs Tyrrell? You might be saved much annoyance and worry.

GR. You are both so kind—I should like to for a little while, certainly. This house has become unbearable of late with debts and difficulties on every side.

LADY S. Oh dear, how terrible. You had better leave at once, Grace. Perhaps you might have some of your things seized. Anyhow, bring with you those that you most value. We will take care of them.

GR. Thanks, Lilian.

LORD S. Well then, that is agreed, Mrs Tyrrell. I am so glad we may be of use to you.

LADY S. We shall expect you this evening, dear.

GR. Yes, I shall get ready at once.

LADY S. And it is time for us to return home. Good-bye, Mr Ussher.

USS. Good-bye, Lady Shrule.

LORD S. Good-bye.

[*Exeunt* LADY SHRULE, GRACE TYRRELL, *and*
LORD SHRULE *by door at right.*

77

Uss. (*gloomily*). Heaven help her — help them all. What is to be done?—Stay—I might go security, I would do anything to help them.—But would it really be of use? Other difficulties must follow these, so that my whole fortune would not suffice. I will think the matter over.—I wonder how the heather field is going on. No one seems to have been there lately.

KIT TYRRELL, *carrying a small white bundle, enters through door at back.*

KIT (*placing the bundle on sofa*). Barry, the pony is splendid.   I had such galloping over the heather field.

Uss. Well, did you bring back any flowers?

KIT. They have not yet come out. All I could find there were these little buds in my handkerchief. (*Unties the bundle*) Look.

Uss. (*with a start*). What — buds of heather? Has your father seen these, Kit?

KIT. Yes, I told him I found them growing all over the heather field.

Uss. You did, boy—and what did he say?

KIT. Nothing for a while. But he looked—he looked —well, I have never seen him look like that before.

Uss. Ha—and then—?

KIT. Oh, then he seemed to forget all about it. He became so kind, and oh, Barry, what do you think, he called me, his " little brother Miles." So I am really his brother, he says, after all—

MILES TYRRELL, *in haste and violent trepidation, enters through door at back.*

MIL. Barry, for pity's sake—(*sees KIT and suddenly*

checks himself, then brings Ussher *over to fireplace*).
Barry, something dreadful has come over Carden. He
does not know me.

Uss. (*in a trembling voice, as he gazes fixedly before
him*). The vengeance of the heather field.

Mil. Oh! for pity's sake, come to him. Come to
him—

Uss. Where is he?

Mil. Wandering helpless about the garden. Oh,
heavens, what shall we do?

Uss. (*with suppressed terror*). Let us find him. (*He
turns to go.*)

Carden Tyrrell *appears outside doorway at back.
He has a strange, collected look.*

Uss. (*starting*). Carden!

Tyr. (*coming in*). Well, Barry?—Why, what has
happened to you since yesterday? My goodness, you
look at least ten years older. (*Glancing at* Miles)
Who is that? He was annoying me about something
just now in the fuchsia walk.

Mil. Oh, I cannot stand this torture. Carden, dear
Carden, look at me—

Tyr. (*retreats like a frightened animal towards* Ussher,
keeping always his eyes fixed on Miles). Barry, what is
the matter with him? Don't leave me alone with him,
Barry. Get him to go away.

Uss. You need not fear him, Carden. (*He signs to*
Miles, *who retires with an inconsolable expression and
stands by fireplace.*)

Tyr. (*after a moment, mysteriously*). Barry—

Uss. Yes, Carden.

Tyr. (*looking cautiously around*). You remember our conversation yesterday.

Uss. (*puzzled*). Yesterday ? I did not see you yesterday.

Tyr. (*with impatience*). We did not walk together on the cliff yesterday, when you advised me not to marry Grace Desmond ? What do you mean ?

Uss. (*suddenly recollecting*). Oh, I remember, I remember. (*Then in a trembling voice*) But Carden— Carden, that was ten years ago. Don't you know that you are now married to her ?

Tyr. (*with a surprised baffled look*). I am ?—

Uss. (*very gently*). Yes, indeed.

Tyr. Oh ! (*His expression for a moment grows vaguely painful, then gradually passes into one of vacant calm. After a short pause*) Barry, you are quite right.

Uss. (*joyfully*). I knew you would understand me, Carden.

Tyr. Yes, I will take your advice. I will not ask her to be my wife.

Uss. (*with cruel disappointment*). Hopeless—I see it is hopeless now.

Tyr. (*unheeding*). I do not care for her any more. I know now I never cared for her.

Uss. Do you ? Why ?

Tyr. (*distressfully*). Oh, I have had such a dreadful dream.

Uss. A dream ?

Tyr. I must tell it to you.—Let me see, what was it ? No—I cannot remember—no,—it has gone completely from me before the beauty of the morning. (*Looks out at back and stretches his arms*) Oh, is not this Spring morning divine ?

Uss. But—Carden, can you not see that it is evening?

Tyr. Ah, I must have been a long time asleep—a long, long time. Yet it looks like the morning. Yes, it seems as if it would always be morning now for me.

Uss. (*with interest*). Indeed—is that so?

Tyr. Yes—its genius somehow is always about me.

Uss. And what do you call this genius of the morning?

Tyr. (*with a strange ecstacy*). Joy! Joy!

Uss. (*after looking at him for a while in wonder*). Then, you are happy, Carden?

Tyr. Oh, yes—so happy. Why not?

Uss. (*with hesitation*). You have no troubles, have you?

Tyr. Troubles—? No, except sometimes in dreams —but oh, when I awake to the joy of this great beauty—

Uss. Yet—great beauty—is it not for ever far away?

Tyr. No—it is for ever by me. (*Then as if suddenly recollecting*) Ah, now I can tell you my dreadful dream. (*Slowly*) I dreamed that my lot was to wander through common luxurious life—seeing now and then in glimpses, that beauty—but so far away! And when the vision left me—ah, you do not know the anguish I felt in looking again at my lot in life.

Uss. And this was only a dream?

Tyr. (*fervently*). Thank heaven—only a dream! (*He goes to the sofa, where* Kit *all this time has been playing with the heather buds.*)

Uss. (*meditatively sorrowful*). And are beauty and happiness mere illusions after all? (*Goes towards* Miles) I am dazed in the presence of this awful misfortune.

Mil. (*approaching* Ussher). Oh, the misery of seeing him like this. He thinks he is living in the old days.

F
81

Uss. It has come upon him again—that eerie ethereal youth I remember so well.

MIL. And for which he would yearn with such fond regret. But Grace and the child— Oh, what is to become of them? I fear their ruin is now certain and complete.

Uss. (*as if suddenly awakened*). Not so.—It may be possible to save them now that there is no danger of further expenditure. And I *will* save them. I will be security for the payment of all their debts. I will save the estate, if it costs me every penny I have in the world.

MIL. (*grasping* USSHER *by the hand*). Oh, Barry, this is good of you. (*They go towards the fireplace in earnest discourse.*)

TYR. (*placing a heather wreath on* KIT's *head*). There —you are like a young field-faun now.

KIT. What sort of thing is that?

TYR. Why, one of the field-fairies fresh and clean as those soft heather-shoots around your hair.

KIT (*delighted*). What—the fairies that live in green hillocks, and dance by the river bank, in the valley over there? Oh, tell me of them again.

TYR. Yes, beautiful child-fairies that play with the water nymphs—those sirens, you know, who sing in the wistful depths of the stream. (*With a sudden transport*) Oh, we must go to Lorlei as last year, where the river is lit with their gold. (*Pointing out at back*) See, even now the sky is darkening as in that storm scene of the old legend I told you on the Rhine. See, the rain across a saffron sun trembles like gold harp strings, through the purple Irish Spring!

ACT III. THE HEATHER FIELD

Mrs Grace Tyrrell *enters by door at right, dressed for going out, with her face thinly veiled and looking altogether younger and more handsome.*

Gr. (*to* Tyrrell). I am just starting to visit the Shrules for some days.

Tyr. (*turns surprised*). Miss Desmond— Oh— (*With emotion and signs of struggle*) Oh, where is that beauty now—that music of the morning? (*Suddenly arrested*) Such strange solemn harmonies. (*Listens.*) The voices —yes, they are filling the house — those white-stoled children of the morning. (*His eyes after a moment wander slowly to the doorway at back*) Oh, the rainbow! (*To* Kit) Come quick, see the lovely rainbow! (*They go to watch it hand in hand.*) Oh, mystic highway of man's speechless longings! My heart goes forth upon the rainbow to that horizon of joy! (*With a fearful exaltation*) The voices—I hear them now triumphant in a silver glory of song!

Gr. (*looking bewildered from* Miles *to* Ussher). What—what is all this?

Uss. Ah, your fears have come true, Mrs Tyrrell. You have not heard——

Gr. No.—What has happened? For heavens' sake, speak.

Uss. The wild heath has broken out again in the heather field.

THE END.

MAEVE

———

A PSYCHOLOGICAL DRAMA IN TWO ACTS

DRAMATIS PERSONÆ

THE O'HEYNES, *Colman O'Heynes, Prince of Burren.*

MAEVE O'HEYNES, } *his daughters.*
FINOLA O'HEYNES, }

HUGH FITZ WALTER, *a young Englishman.*

PEG INERNY, *a vagrant.*

In the dream of MAEVE appear QUEEN MAEVE, A BOY PAGE, CHORUS OF BOY PAGES, ancient Irish harpers, chieftains, warriors, people, etc.

The action takes place during the present time about and at O'Heynes Castle among the Burren Mountains of County Clare in Ireland.

ACT I

A ruined abbey in a green valley among mountains covered with layers of grey rock. At back a little removed is a cairn overgrown with grass. Gray limestones belonging to the ruin are strewn about the ground. At the left in the surrounding pasture of pale green, great leafless ash trees stand among boulders spotted with white and orange lichen. It is a sunny evening in the month of March.

(MAEVE O'HEYNES—a girl of about three and twenty with a fair complexion, gold hair, and a certain boyish beauty in the lines and movement of her slim figure, rests thoughtful and attentive on one of the fallen stones. She wears a red frieze dress with a black jacket and folding linen collar, and has on her head a sailor's cap of black wool.)

(FINOLA O'HEYNES—a dark rather submissive-looking girl somewhat younger, dressed simply in an ordinary gown, sits near on another stone.)

FINOLA (*reading from an old book*).—
    "Every hill which is at this Oenach
    Hath under it heroes and queens,
    And poets and distributors,
    And fair fierce women."

MAEVE (*rises and gazes before her as if in a dream*). And fair fierce women!

FIN. (*closing the book, goes to her*). Maeve—what are you thinking of so earnestly?

MA. (*recalled to herself*). Visions—visions.—That is all.

87

FIN. Has this old West Connacht poem brought you visions?

MA. Ah, the bard Dorban, who wrote it, was a poet! (*She sighs and covers her face with her hands.*)

FIN. (*turning away*). I am sorry I thought of reading it to you.

MA. Why, sister?

FIN. Because it seems to have called you back to your old self.

MA. (*smiling sadly*). My old self. As if I could ever have left my old self.

FIN. Oh yes, you were peaceful and contented a little while ago.

MA. It seems so long ago, Finola.

FIN. Something strange has come over you now.

MA. (*with restlessness*). No, it is nothing. It is only the look of the evening.

FIN. But this is such a peaceful evening with that saffron sunlight over the ruins. Why should it make you anything else but peaceful?

MA. Oh, Finola, when I see the ruins like that, I know the visions are near me.

FIN. Then, after all, it was not because I read that poem?

MA. Yes—that, and the evening.

FIN. (*looking at her anxiously*). Why should the visions make you so sad, Maeve?

MA. (*wistfully*). Such beautiful dead people! They used to walk in the oldest of these ruins before it was a ruin ; they watched Goban, the great architect, building that round tower (*pointing to the right*), building his master-work. I see them now, and I see others who lived long before them (*turns and looks to the back*), and are buried in that green cairn. Oh, I am dying because I am exiled from such beauty.

FIN. (*with great gentleness*). Darling, you must not think of these things. You know to-morrow——

MA. (*with a sudden chillness*). To-morrow,—why do you speak of to-morrow while it is still to-day, and I can still think of my love ?

FIN. *To*-morrow when you are married, Maeve, it will be your husband who will be entitled to that love.

MA. (*significantly*). He has not yet returned.

FIN. Hugh will certainly return before night.

MA. But he has not yet returned, Finola.

FIN. Do you really think he will not return ?

MA. (*with a baffled look*). Oh, I don't know : but some-how I cannot believe that I am to be married to-morrow. (*Looks around*) To leave all this for an English home—

FIN. (*with increased anxiety*). Maeve—

MA. The very stones, as I wander among them, seem to forbid it.   [*Exit among the ruins at back.*

FIN. (*walking about in agitation*). Oh, why does not Hugh return ? (*Then suddenly stopping*) Here is father again. Poor father.

THE O'HEYNES *enters from the left, leaning heavily on a stick. He is an old man, with thin, white dishevelled hair almost falling to his shoulders, wears a tall hat and clothes of a somewhat bygone fashion; while about his whole appearance there is just a suggestion of the peasant.*

THE O'H. (*restlessly*). Finola, I wonder will Hugh come after all ?

FIN. Of course he will, father. Why have you been asking me this question all day?

THE O'H. Because he has been promising to come for ever so long, and he has not come.

FIN. Well—you know the reason.

THE O'H. (*peevishly*). Yes—yes—legal business— always the same excuse.

FIN. You surely must understand that he had to consult the lawyers about many matters before his marriage with Maeve.

THE O'H. When he left here for England he said it would only be for a little time, and here he has been away more than two months.

FIN. The delay was very unfortunate, but necessary, I suppose. You see every sort of legal business is so tedious.

THE O'H. I don't know—I don't know. I distrust his excuses. He said he would certainly return to-day, and there, he hasn't after all.

FIN. But to-day is not yet over. Oh, you needn't fear. He will return before to-morrow.

THE O'H. Ah, this is the way you are perpetually making excuses for him, Finola.

FIN. (*a little confused*). Father, why do you say so?

THE O'H. I understand it all. Another girl would not be so forgiving as you are, Finola.

FIN. I have nothing to forgive.

THE O'H. That is well, child. But, believe me, I had far rather he had married you than Maeve.

FIN. Oh, no. He always liked Maeve from the first, and no one else. I never at any time doubted that, father.

THE O'H. Well, this is certainly a queer way of showing his affection for her.

FIN. I suppose it would be, if there were no reasons for it.

THE O'H. (*indignantly*). To think he should have put off coming until his very wedding morning. He deserves to lose her after leaving her all this time. Oh the persistent ill-luck that has pursued me all through life.

FIN. I'm sure I can't think how you consider it ill-luck to be on the eve of having all your wishes fulfilled.

THE O'H. Ah, that is just it, child. I have so often been on the eve of having my wishes fulfilled: and then somehow the unforeseen has come about: and all my hopes have gone from me. I am surely the most unfortunate of men.

FIN. Father, dear, you must not despond in this way.

THE O'H. To think of all the anxiety your sister has caused me, Finola, and the trouble she put me to before she would accept this rich young Englishman. She must have been mad. As if the coming into this place of such a suitor was an everyday event to her.

FIN. (*pensively*). He never for a moment interested her somehow. It was very strange, his coming—wasn't it?

THE O'H. Was there ever such good fortune? I advertise the fishing of my river in the papers. He arrives here last summer, and takes it at once. To be sure it is splendid salmon fishing—but that it should have brought such a tenant as Hugh Fitz Walter—and that he should have fallen in love with Maeve—well—

FIN. (*with a sigh*). Well, father, you ought to be content with such good fortune.

THE O'H. (*despondingly*). Ah, I am afraid it is too

good to come to anything. But just think that after all *he* should be the one to wreck this good fortune—Oh, I am distracted. (*He begins to work his hands and tear his hair.*)

FIN. (*alarmed*). Father, don't fret in this way. It is bad for your health. And you know there is no reason for it.

THE O'H. (*feebly*). Oh child, if you could only realise how I have waited and waited for this—for the time when fortune would enable our family to resume its fitting position in the county! Hugh has at last promised me this fortune. Is it surprising that I should be anxious, when I see the danger of his failing me?

FIN. (*inadvertently*). He is not the one who will fail you, father.

THE O'H. (*with a quick suspicion*). You think Maeve is more likely to—eh? Where is she?

FIN. Oh don't trouble about her. She is safe.

THE O'H. I noticed she was taking to her old habits lately. I had again to forbid her to wander through the country at night.

FIN. (*as if laughing the matter off*). You must not mind these wanderings of hers. They are very harmless, father.

THE O'H. (*anxiously*). Does she still talk of this strange one she is in love with?

FIN. Oh that is nothing. Don't trouble about it.

THE O'H. I am not so sure of what you say, Finola. I'll take my oath she is thinking about some good for nothing fellow after all.

FIN. No—no, nothing of the kind. You don't understand her.

THE O'H. Indeed I don't, child.

FIN. It is not often easy to do so. She seems to live by the brain as we live by the heart.

THE O'H. She seems to me quite regardless of realities.

FIN. Those feelings and impulses which are in our hearts and which govern our affections, with her are all in the head. This sounds strange: but it is the only way I can account for her nature.

THE O'H. (*surprised*). In the head?

FIN. Yes—that is why she appears so cold, and, as you say, regardless of realities. I even think if this one she loves were to become a reality, he would cease to fascinate her.

THE O'H. (*curiously*). Have you ever found out who he is?

FIN. No—not altogether.

THE O'H. I wonder what put such an extravagant idea in her head.

FIN. I think I know.

THE O'H. Well, what is it?

FIN. Would you believe it, father, I think it is those books that belonged to Uncle Bryan.

THE O'H. You mean those books up in the top room. They are mostly about ancient Greece, aren't they?

FIN. Yes. She is always poring over them and looking at their pictures—white statues and beautiful wall ornaments which she told me were in Greece. And then she showed me other books too, with pictures of pillars and arches—all ornamented like those in the abbey here. Then I have seen her take the writings of Uncle Bryan and study them with all these pictures before her.

THE O'H. Poor Bryan's writings, do you say? I didn't

think there were any here. I thought the Society he belonged to, took them all. (*With plaintive regret*) My poor brother Bryan ; he was a great scholar. They used to talk of him in Dublin. They said if he had lived to complete his book, it would have made him famous.

FIN. What was he writing about when he died, father ?

THE O'H. Let me see—I think his work was to be called "The Influence of Greek Art on Celtic Ornament" or something of the sort.

FIN. That must have been it ; for Maeve is always talking of that, and of the brotherhood of the Greek and Celtic races, and of a curious unreal beauty besides, which she says the Greeks invented. She thinks she has discovered something similar in the Celt.

THE O'H. Is that what you say she is in love with ?

FIN. (*with earnest conviction*). I verily believe so, father. (*Then after a moment's consideration*) Still it often seems to me she must have some individual in her mind besides.

THE O'H. I thought that was the case.

FIN. Oh—not what you think.

THE O'H. What then, child ?

FIN. I don't know ;—she speaks of his beauty as if it had some sort of likeness to the Celtic ornament she is so much in love with.

THE O'H. Ah, she must have discovered this in the writings of Bryan.—He had all sorts of odd theories about everything, poor fellow.

FIN. Yes, and she is as full of theories. She says that, because Celtic ornament is as rare and delicate as the Greek, so her pattern of Celtic youth must, in the same way, equal the perfection of Greek youth.

MAEVE

THE O'H. (*astonished*). My goodness, is the whole of life like this to her?

FIN. Ah, now you understand what I meant when I told you that everything with her seemed to be only in the head.

THE O'H. (*seriously*). Yes, Finola, and nothing in the heart. She has no warm feelings of the heart. She was always cold and distant from her earliest childhood.

FIN. No, I would not say so much. I think it is only her imagination that has absorbed all the warmth of her nature.

THE O'H. What you say is the same thing, my dear. Whatever may be the cause, depend upon it, she has no feeling.

FIN. Oh, don't say that, father.

THE O'H. Oh no, she hasn't, Finola ; and I don't wonder that this young man's affection should at last weary of her apathy.

FIN. It is not any want of affection that has delayed him, father.

THE O'H. I cannot believe any more in his affection. (*Querulously*) Why is he not here? Why is he not here?

FIN. You will surely see him very soon. For goodness sake, do not fret so. Go in, and try and rest.

THE O'H. Rest—I cannot rest. How can I rest with this anxiety gnawing at me?

FIN. Oh, this miserable pride and position. They are ruining your health and peace.

THE O'H. (*with a sudden reviving of energy*). Not they, my girl, indeed—why do you say so? Why should what are good for every other man be bad for old Colman O'Heynes?

FIN. Yes, yes, father dear, I know. But somehow we have been so happy and united in our seclusion here. We are going to be divided.

THE O'H. How divided?

FIN. Maeve will soon leave us.

THE O'H. Ah—yes, of course.

FIN. Let that be sufficient. Let us at least not try to go out into the world.

THE O'H. Why not, Finola?

FIN. The world is such a great lonely place.

THE O'H. But my lost position—the lost dignity of our family. I have that to reassert. When my rich son-in-law comes there will be an end of our poverty.

FIN. You are the Prince of Burren.—Is not the royalty of our race acknowledged? What place can *we* find in a grotesque world of plutocrats and shop-keeper peers? This change in our life seems unnatural to me. And then that wicked old Peg Inerny is always talking.

THE O'H. (*sharply*). Eh—what does she say?

FIN. Oh, nothing definite—nothing but insinuations and mystery, till I feel quite terrified.

THE O'H. She has been the curse of our house; and now the infernal witch has bewitched your sister.

FIN. I don't think that—I hope not. Maeve is only fascinated by her strange tales—the past, always the past.

THE O'H. Ay, it was the same way with your poor mother and this Peg Inerny who was a servant here long ago, and put it into her head to call your sister by the name of Maeve. Peg Inerny, I know, had some sinister object for this.

FIN. Oh, no, no.

THE O'H. Ah—wait a while.

Fin. (*with a scared look*). Father, don't forebode evil. Try and be contented—try and check this restlessness that is urging you to change your life.   Let us go in. (*As they move to the left*) Look at our old castle.   How spectral those giant ash trees rise up around it from the pale March grass.   How peaceful they all live in the sunset.   Would it not be misery to leave that peace for a world where there is at least no peace.

Hugh Fitz Walter—*a good-looking young English-man of about five and twenty, dressed in a tweed suit—enters at the right.*

Hugh (*eagerly*). So I have arrived, you see, at last.

The O'H. (*turning*). Who is that?—what, Hugh?

Hugh. It is I.

The O'H. And so it is.—Heaven be praised.   I thought you were never coming, Hugh. (*He shakes him by the hand.*)

Fin. (*also shaking him by the hand*). I am so glad you have come—at last.

Hugh. But I wrote to you my reason for not getting here sooner.

The O'H. Yes, I know, of course.   But why should you have put off coming like this till the very last?

Hugh. Haven't I explained to you again and again how my affairs delayed me?

The O'H. (*peevishly*). Yes—yes—explanations.   You have caused me, Hugh, the greatest anxiety for all that.

Hugh. I assure you, O'Heynes, this delay was sorely against my will: and I am sorry you have had any anxiety on my account.   Why you have, indeed, I cannot understand.

G   97

THE O'H. My mind has been a prey to all sorts of doubts and forebodings.

HUGH (*alarmed*). Good gracious. What is this for? Isn't Maeve well? How is she?

THE O'H. (*impatiently*). Oh, she is well—well enough.

HUGH. You are hiding something from me, O'Heynes.

THE O'H. No—not at all.

HUGH. I, too, was anxious. That is why I hurried here at once after my arrival in the village.

THE O'H. (*suspiciously*). Eh—why were you anxious?

HUGH. I had not heard about her from Finola for some days.

THE O'H. There is nothing the matter with her except what has come by your protracted absence.

HUGH (*frightened*). What has come to her? You alarm me.

THE O'H. Only a return of her strange ways that used to trouble me before her engagement to you. That is all.

HUGH (*with visible relief*). Oh—that is all.

THE O'H. (*involuntarily*). She frightens me sometimes.

HUGH. In what way?

THE O'H. (*hesitates and looks confused*).

FIN. Oh, don't worry her about such things. Hush, here she comes.

MAEVE O'HEYNES *enters from the back.*

HUGH. Oh, Maeve, what is it—?

MA. (*starts when she perceives him*).

HUGH (*goes eagerly to her, but is checked by the chillness of her manner, then taking her hand which she gives apathetically*). I hope you are not angry, Maeve. I came as soon as it was possible for me.

MA. (*with some recovered composure*). Oh—for that—I am not angry in the least—I am not angry at all.

HUGH. You looked as if something disturbed you.

FIN. Hugh, it is only her surprise at suddenly seeing you.

THE O'H. Yes, indeed, when you have disappointed her so often. But, thank heaven, you have arrived safe at last. Come, Finola, come, now I can rest. I feel I want rest after all this suspense. Come, let us go indoors.

[*Exeunt* THE O'HEYNES *and* FINOLA O'HEYNES *at left.*

HUGH (*to* MAEVE). Well, I am back at last; and you—you are so silent and forgetful there among those old stones.

MA. (*as if recalled to herself*). No. I am in reality thinking of this very thing.

HUGH. Of my coming?

MA. Yes.

HUGH. It has no interest for you one way or the other?

MA. Oh yes. But I can not understand father's reason for being so troubled about it.

HUGH. Of course not. As if I wouldn't return on the first opportunity to you. Why do you seem annoyed that I should tell you this?

MA. (*restlessly*). Somehow there seem such cross purposes in this world of ours.

HUGH. Cross purposes—how so?

MA. Oh I don't know—persons seem to give others what those others don't want from them, but want from someone else.

HUGH. That is indeed a world of cross purposes.

MA. (*sadly*). Don't you see that it is just so with us here?

HUGH. (*dejectedly*). You mean that I give what is not wanted.

MA. Yes, and that another would give you what you want from some one else.

HUGH. Who is that other?

MA. The one whom you once appeared to like best.

HUGH. You are the one I always liked best in the world.

MA. The world did not think so.

HUGH. Indeed?—You puzzle me. Explain what you are saying?

MA. (*with a certain embarrassment*). I thought you liked my sister better than me.

HUGH. Than you? Oh no—impossible. I know you don't believe what you are saying.

MA. But you appeared to be so much more intimate with her than you have been with me.

HUGH. Ah, that is just it. I have the greatest affection for Finola. I admire her goodness and unselfishness. She has indeed the disposition of an angel.

MA. And yet you could leave her for one so less worthy, as I am.

HUGH. You shall not say you are less worthy; I can see no fault in you.

MA. Oh, why did you ever leave Finola?

HUGH. You forget we were never more than friends. She is one of my very dearest friends.

MA. And you were never engaged to her?

HUGH. Never. It was only when I despaired of your consent that I thought for a while of Finola. But it was no use. Your image always rose up between us. I soon understood that for me you were the only one in the world. (*Pause.*)

MA. (*absently*). The only one in the world. What happiness it must be to find the one who is so much as that.

HUGH. It may also be misery—that is, in a certain sense.

MA. (*a little surprised*). Really? How can it be misery?

HUGH. When we know that nothing of what we feel is returned.

MA. (*abstractedly*). I should not have thought that much mattered.

HUGH. Do you say this because I persist in loving you through all your contempt of my love?

MA. Oh no—I was not thinking of you at all.

HUGH. What was your reason then for saying it?

MA. (*with a pensive deliberation*). I should have imagined that if one really loved, one would shrink from a return of love.

HUGH. (*surprised*). You wouldn't like your love returned?

MA. Ah no, for I think if it were, the beauty of love would come to an end in the lover.

HUGH. How very strange. But why should I think so? Yours is the reasoning of one who has never known love.

MA. So you think I have never known love?

HUGH. Certainly. (*Pause.*) Have you?

MA. Well, I can tell you truly that I have.

HUGH (*in a serious tone*). Is that really so?

MA. Yes.

HUGH (*with a sudden suspicion*). Do you love some one now?

MA. (*quietly*). Yes.

HUGH (*growing excited*). Who is he?

MA. (*wearily*). Oh, what is the use of telling you?

HUGH. Who is he, I say? For pity's sake speak.

MA. You would never understand.

HUGH (*bitterly*). I should understand only too well.

MA. Look around you, then.

HUGH (*puzzled, looking around him*). Well? I see no one.

MA. (*scornfully*). I knew you would not understand.

HUGH (*wondering*). I see nothing but these ruins—that mysterious round tower—the stony mountains—and your gray castle through the leafless boughs of great ash trees.

MA. (*with a visionary look in her eyes*). And you see nothing but these?

HUGH. Oh, what is this mystery? Will you tell me?

MA. (*smiling ecstatically*). Among all these that you see —listen to what Gráinne says in the old poem—

    "There lives a one
        On whom I would love to gaze long,
        For whom I would give the whole world,
        All, all, though it is a delusion."

HUGH (*downcast*). You are mocking me.

MA. (*gently*). Oh, no.—How can you think so? Are not all things beautiful that remind us of our love?

HUGH (*after looking at her calmly for some time*). Yes, you are right. How strange you are. I do not understand you. Among us simple men you seem like one of your golden fairies. What is the name you call them?

MA. Túatha dê Danann, those tall beautiful children of

the Dagda Môr. It is said they were the old people
of Erin and were afterwards worshipped as gods.

HUGH. But you do not believe they are really gods?

MA. Oh, no—only a race whose great beauty still haunts
our land. (*Sadly*) They were too beautiful to compare
with me.

HUGH. They could not be more beautiful than you are.
You don't know how beautiful you are to me. No—if
you knew, you would not be so indifferent. Ah, I realise
but too well how little you care for me. You would
never have consented to be my wife but for your father:
you are doing it all for your father—not for me.

MA. Oh, why do you go back to all that? Have I not
consented? And is not that the main thing?

HUGH (*resignedly*). Yes,—I suppose I must be satisfied.
I must only trust to time for winning you completely.

MA. (*with mysterious significance*). Let us all trust to
time.

HUGH (*brightening*). May I put my trust in time?

MA. You must ask that question of Time himself.

HUGH. Oh, I am confident of his answer.

MA. And I too, am confident in Time.

[*Exeunt leisurely at the left.*

As they are going, PEG INERNY—*a little old woman in a
    ragged red frieze petticoat, a black frieze cloak raised
    up to partially cover her head, and with dark woollen
    stockings worn away at the bare soles of her feet—
    enters stealthily from among the ruins at back.
    Muttering indistinctly she follows the two for a
    while, then squats down on a stone and gazes fixedly
    at the cairn.*

After a pause MAEVE *and* FINOLA O'HEYNES *enter at the left.*

FIN. Oh, Maeve, why do you come out here again?

MA. (*joyfully*). He is gone. Until to-morrow, at least I shall be free.

FIN. Poor Hugh.

MA. He is gone; and I will make the most of my little liberty. I have to say good-bye to beauty. How this moonlit night—this Irish night comes like a fawn!

FIN. (*perceives* PEG INERNY *and stands as if transfixed*).

MA. What's the matter, Finola? (*Turns and looks*) Oh, it is only Peg Inerny.

FIN. Come away, Maeve, for heavens' sake come. I have left father sleeping in the hall; and if he awakes he is sure to call me, and ask where you are.

MA. (*not heeding* FINOLA). Peg, Peg, I have not seen you for many days. What has brought you here to-night?

PEG (*rousing herself slowly and looking steadily at* MAEVE). I come to take a last farewell of my Princess on the night before her wedding day.

MA. (*with a rigid melancholy*). Yes, I shall never return here, Peg.

PEG. Do you think you will ever leave, Princess?

FIN. Oh, what is that she says? I am terrified.

MA. (*carelessly*). You are always alarmed at one thing or another, Finola.

FIN. (*uneasily*). No—no—but didn't you hear her?

PEG. (*to* FINOLA). Princess, do not fear a poor old woman.

FIN. Why will you always call us princesses?

PEG. Isn't your father a prince? The Prince of Burren?

MA. (*impatiently*). A prince indeed. It is a mockery now to call him that.

PEG. The O'Heynes is none the less a prince whatever he may have done to put shame on his race.

MA. (*helplessly*). Oh, what a misfortune it was.

FIN. (*expostulating*). Maeve—darling.

PEG (*slyly*). They told me my Princess Maeve was content to marry her young Englishman.

MA. (*with suppressed scorn*). Ha—no one ever troubled before to consider whether she was or not.

PEG. He is so rich—so rich with his grand English house and possessions.

MA. Yes indeed—and that is how the whole tragedy has come about.

PEG. I was sure you cared not, Princess, for this world's riches.

MA. (*sadly*). Heaven knows I never had any greed of them.

FIN. Oh Maeve, I thought you had done with these complaints once and for all.

MA. (*pained and irresolute*). So I, too, thought—once perhaps. But to-day in the abbey—it was so beautiful. Something seemed to come back to me.

PEG. It was haunting you, Princess? The day-ghost, eh?

MA. (*with a wan look*). The day-ghost. Oh the wistful pleading of a day-ghost!

FIN. (*frightened*). Why do you say that, Maeve?

MA. Ah — if you saw him — but you never have, Finola.

Fin. Saw him—good heavens, where?

Ma. (*pointing to the round tower*). In the master-work of Goban—in the mountains too.

Peg. Your love is dreaming among the rocks of these mountains, Princess.

Ma. (*with a sort of ecstacy*). Oh, how I have grown to love these stony mountains.

Peg. They are the pleasure haunts of many a beautiful ghost.

Ma. The many beautiful buried in that cairn.

Peg. Oh what a world there is underneath that cairn.

Ma. (*pensively*). Yes, the great beautiful Queen Maeve who reigned over Connacht hundreds of years ago—she is buried in that cairn you say?

Peg. Haven't I often told you so, Princess?

Fin. But I have always understood that Queen Maeve was buried at Rathcroghan in County Roscommon.

Peg. No, Princess, she is here.

Fin. (*inquiringly*). Can you know that?

Peg. Can I know? I can know many things. (*With a low laugh*) Indeed I ought to know where Queen Maeve is.

Ma. Why you especially, Peg?

Peg. Haven't I dwelt in her palace, child?

Fin. (*timidly approaching* Maeve). That is a strange thing to say.

Peg. (*continuing with a sort of inward satisfaction*). Yes, I have dwelt in her palace. Ha—ha—does anyone think that I could bear my miserable outcast life in the world if I could not live the other life also? Oh, my sweet ladies, you don't know the grandeur of that other life.

MA. (*eagerly*). Tell me, do tell me of that other life.

FIN. Maeve—take care—don't ask such a thing.

MA. (*impatiently*). Oh Finola, you mustn't prevent me in this way. (*To* PEG INERNY) Tell me.

PEG. A life among the people with beautiful looks.

MA. (*suddenly delighted*). With beautiful looks!

PEG. Yes, Princess—Oh, just so graceful and clean as you are yourself. I often think you must be one of them.

MA. Tell me more about those people.

PEG. They are now ruled over by the great Queen Maeve.

MA. (*puzzled*). But—she is dead, isn't she? Didn't you say she was buried in the cairn?

PEG (*with an enigmatical grimace*). Yes, yes, Princess —but not dead—Oh, I never said that she was dead.

MA. What new and wonderful tale are you now telling me?

PEG. Haven't I told you before that Queen Maeve has ever been watchful of you?

MA. (*surprised*). No—you have not. What does this mean?

PEG. Just fancy, Princess, it was she who had you called after herself.

FIN. (*excitedly*). Maeve, don't believe her. How is this possible?

PEG. Ah, Princess Finola, didn't you ever know that I was once a servant in the Castle?

FIN. (*restraining herself*). Yes, I believe you were. It was a very long time ago, was it not?

PEG. When your beautiful sister here was born.

FIN. Well then, supposing you were, what has that to do with Queen Maeve naming my sister?

PEG (*slyly*). Oh—only 'twas I made them think of calling her Maeve.

FIN. But you said Queen Maeve did so?

PEG (*with veiled significance*). Haven't I told you of the other life I lead, sweet Princess Finola?

FIN. (*starts, then looking awed and mystified at* PEG INERNY, *says in a trembling voice*) Maeve, she is a wicked woman. It is not right to hold any intercourse with her.

MA. (*who has been listening with a troubled expression*). Ah me, I am the most miserable one in the world.

FIN. (*terrified*). Dearest, for pity's sake don't—don't give way to such a feeling.

MA. (*despairingly*). My father—oh, my father.

PEG. I know it was for his sake alone that you promised to marry this Hugh Fitz Walter.

MA. Yes, father will become rich and great—but my heart will break.

FIN. (*anxiously*). No—no, Maeve, you must remember how good and kind Hugh is. He will surely never cause you unhappiness.

MA. How could he be anything but unhappiness to me, when I can only think of my beloved?

PEG (*insidiously*). That one who haunts the mountains and the beautiful old buildings, Princess—

MA. My beloved whom I am leaving for ever!

FIN. (*throwing her arms around her sister*). Hush—you must not think of him any more, Maeve.

PEG. Ah—you cling to her like ivy, my Lady Finola. You were the one made for clinging. You were the wife that would have been best for the Englishman.

MA. Oh, if he could but understand that this is so.

PEG. They never can, Princess. Dwellers in the valley are always looking at the heights above them.

MA. (*sadly*). I am no longer on those heights. I have fallen from them miserably, and have become (*looking at* FINOLA) like the ivy in the valley.

PEG. Not yet—you are still on the heights. No, you are still like the tall smooth larch on the top of the mountain.

MA. (*dejectedly*). Ah, no, not any longer.

PEG. Come then, to the mountains, Princess—there you will believe it.

FIN. (*restraining her*). Maeve, Maeve, do not go. It will kill father if he hears you have wandered away to-night.

PEG. See how bright it is. The night is lit for your visit. (MAEVE *appears to hesitate*.) Beware of the ivy clinging around the larch, Princess Maeve. It will kill the fairy growth of the larch.

MA. (*restlessly*). Let me go, Finola, let me go.

FIN. I will not, Maeve.

MA. Let me go to the mountains for this last time; I promise to return soon.

FIN. Oh, sister, do not go there to-night.

MA. How white the moon rays dance upon the mountains.

PEG. It is the mountains, Princess, that are white with the dancing feet of the fairies.

MA. (*desperately*). I must go there to-night.

FIN. You shall not, Maeve.

MA. (*gazing fondly on the mountains*). Oh beauty of my day-dreams come forth from the mountains.

PEG. Princess, what is it that you see?

MA. (*with transport*). My love, like an exhalation from the earth to the stars!

PEG (*moving towards the back*). Come, Princess, come.
MA. I am coming.

FIN. (*with a sudden determination*). Then I shall go
too. I could not bear the suspense of your absence.
(*Distant voice of* THE O'HEYNES *is heard several times
calling* "FINOLA.") Good heavens, there is father
calling (*runs to the left and listens in great agitation
while the calling is repeated*). Yes, father, yes, father.

[*Exeunt* MAEVE O'HEYNES *and* PEG INERNY *quickly
at the back.*

FIN. If he finds she has gone he will be so distressed.
I must not tell him. Oh, Maeve, why, why have you gone?
Yes, father—coming—coming.   [*Exit at left.*

ACT II

The exterior of O'Heynes Castle. At the left a large square
tower with its two roof gables facing right and left, and
Irish battlements which carry two high chimneys, one at
front and one at back of roof. On ground level at front is
the pointed Gothic entrance-door, over which a square-
headed window lights a room above, while on the side facing
the right above a hall window, is another square-headed
window belonging to the same upper room. Around great
leafless ash trees grow upon the pale green grass. Some way
off at the right is the cairn with the abbey ruins beyond; and
stony mountain ranges, as in the first act, form a background
to the whole scene.

It is a frosty night with a very bright moon.

FINOLA O'HEYNES, closely muffled, comes out through the
door of the castle.

FIN. Maeve. Are you there, Maeve? (*Pause.*) Maeve.
(*Goes to the right and peers about*) I don't see any sign of

her. Oh dear, oh dear, I wonder does she intend to come back. (*With an anxious and undecided look*) I don't know which way to search for her. Stop—I will try this path leading to the mountain.

[*Exit at back behind the Castle.*

MAEVE O'HEYNES, *looking very pale and listless, enters from the right.*

MA. (*gazing forlorn around the scene*). Oh, moon and mountain and ruin, give a voice to my infinite sadness! (*Pause.*)

[FINOLA O'HEYNES *re-enters from behind the Castle.*

FIN. O sister, you are here!

MA. (*slowly*). Yes.

FIN. Thank heaven, you have returned. (*She advances towards her.*)

MA. I said I would return, Finola.

FIN. Oh, I was so frightened. Aren't you perished without a cloak on, this bitter night?

MA. (*wearily*). Is it so cold?

FIN. (*surprised*). Cold? You must feel this biting frosty air?

MA. No—not particularly.

FIN. (*feeling the hands and face of* MAEVE). Why, Maeve, you are like ice.

MA. (*as if remembering*). Like ice. How beautiful to be like the ice!

FIN. Oh, come in, come in from the cold.

MA. No—let me wait here, in the moonlight.

FIN. Darling, you will get dreadfully ill—and on your wedding morning too.

111

MA. (*with a shudder*). What—it is not yet the day?

FIN. Midnight has just passed—yes, this is your wedding day.

MA. (*mournfully*). Oh, so soon—so soon.

FIN. Far better had it been sooner, my poor sister.

MA. Oh, don't say that, Finola.

FIN. Yes, yes, this long delay since your engagement has brought the old trouble upon you again.

MA. (*with a scornful smile*). Do you think I was ever really reconciled to my fate?

FIN. And yet—and yet—you seemed happy for a while.

MA. No—never really. I was only talked into a false sort of happiness, Finola.

FIN. (*expostulating*). Oh, how can you say that?

MA. Yes, I deceived myself there among you. You all seemed so happy, and were so kind and indulgent to me, that I wished to believe this marriage was for the best.

FIN. And you never really believed it?

MA. Never—I was soon certain that I never did.

FIN. When was that?

MA. When he went to England to arrange with his lawyers, and this family happiness that encircled me gradually disappeared—

FIN. Do you think so? I am sure father and I have never changed.

MA. Perhaps not, but you understand, I was left more to myself and had time to think over what I had done. (*Despairingly*) Ah then I saw that I never could be reconciled to my fate.

FIN. Darling, you should not have encouraged such a thought. It will leave you, when you are married and away from here.

MA. Oh, the sacrifice—I make it for father's sake.

FIN. Be sure your sacrifice for father's sake will have its reward.

MA. It is a cruel sacrifice. And yet it must be—

FIN. Poor Hugh. At all events he is unchanged.

MA. I too am unchanged, Finola. Don't you see it after what I have told you?

FIN. I suppose so. But have you always disliked him? You do not hate him?

MA. Oh, but if you were to see him, Finola, in the light he appears to me—

FIN. How does he appear to you, dear?

MA. (*with sudden vehemence*). A bandit—a plunderer!

FIN. Maeve, what are you saying?

MA. Yes, I say a bandit, like his English predecessors who ruined every beautiful thing we ever had.

FIN. (*frightened*). Sister, how can you accuse him of that?

MA. (*bitterly*). Yes, he has come finally to ruin every beautiful thing.

FIN. He, who is so generous? Why, instead of destroying, is he not restoring the dignity of our ancient Celtic house?

MA. (*scornfully*). Yes, I know what such restoration means. It is bought at too great a price, I can tell you. It is like that great restoration of a family's pride by Strongbow, who first brought our humiliation upon us.

FIN. No—I cannot see the likeness, Maeve.

MA. Don't you remember the conditions of the English noble whom the Irish king Diarmid called to his aid?

FIN. Was it not, if Strongbow regained for Diarmid his kingdom he was to marry the king's daughter Eva?

MA. Yes, and then become heir to Diarmid.—He succeeded in regaining the kingdom and the conditions were fulfilled, weren't they?

FIN. They were.

MA. And thus with the power that was given him he subdued and ruined the ancient splendour of Erin. The old, old story! Poor Eva, you were sacrificed—a sweet symbol of your country in her subjection.

FIN. That may be, but still I can't understand in what way Hugh is to injure our country.

MA. By killing the last flame of her life.

FIN. The last flame of our country's life? How is that?

MA. Yes, the last light of her life.

FIN. What is this last light?

MA. (*with a child's smile and as if forgetful of all sorrows*). The fairy lamp of Celtic Beauty!

FIN. (*after a moment, in a very gentle voice*). Dearest, it is impossible he ever could do this thing.

MA. Is he not destroying my chosen way of life—that life which alone may keep the flame alight? Am I not the last?

FIN. The last? Why should you think that you are the last?

MA. Listen and I will tell you, Finola. You have heard Peg Inerny speak of her other life, and of having dwelt in the palace of Queen Maeve?

FIN. (*nervously*.) Yes, what of her?

MA. This very night after I had left her upon the mountain I thought I saw her beckoning to me in the abbey. I followed her while she went past the round tower to the cairn which now was glowing against a sky that had turned crimson. With a gesture the old woman seemed to open the cairn, and then stood transformed in a curious region of fresh green suffused with saffron light, so that I saw her tall, and beautiful, and marvellously pale of face, and crowned with a golden diadem not so golden as her hair.   And I heard her say these words in ancient Gaelic :—" Last Princess of Erin, thou art a lonely dweller among strange peoples ; but I the great Queen Maeve have watched thee from thy birth, for thou wert to be the vestal of our country's last beauty.   Behold whom thy love hath called to life.   Mark him well, for already his hour of dissolution hath come."   And I looked and saw him who was beauty standing by the round tower. With a feeling of nothingnéss, I fell upon my knees and bent down to the earth.   When I looked again he was not there.   Then a company of ancient Celts bore a covered form upon their shoulders ; while a choir of rose-crowned boys sang dirges with violet voices of frail, lace-like beauty.   And they buried their dead one by the round tower, and over his grave they raised a great ogham stone. And again I heard the voice of the Queen :—"They have buried thy dead beauty, Princess.   Thou hast killed him by deserting thy chosen way of life ; for there are no more who live for beauty."   Then in my desolation I seemed to lose consciousness of all save these last words of the queen: "Yet, princess, I will come and comfort thee again to-night."   And with a start I discovered that I was sitting alone in the moonlight by the round tower.   And I looked, and I could not find the great ogham stone that they had raised over my beloved.

FIN. And so you were only dreaming after all ?

MA. Yes, it must have only been a dream—for my beloved is not dead.

FIN. Nor will Queen Maeve come to you again to-night.

MA. Do not be so sure of that, Finola.

FIN. (*in a frightened voice*). Oh heavens! there she is.

MA. (*starting*). Who?

FIN. Peg Inerny.

PEG INERNY *enters from the right.*

PEG. My noble ladies.

FIN. (*angrily*). What do you want?

PEG. Oh, I never thought you could be so sharp, Lady Finola.

FIN. (*with the desperation of terror*). Go—you are here for no good purpose.

MA. (*deprecatingly*). Finola.

PEG (*to* FINOLA). Won't you give me the liberty of a wild beast to walk about at night, my dear?

FIN. (*shrieking*). Go, I say, or I will let loose the dogs of the castle upon you.

MA. Finola, for goodness sake, what are you saying? What wrong has she ever done to any of us?

FIN. Oh yes, don't I know her evil intentions towards you?

MA. I feel sure she has never done me harm.

PEG (*to* MAEVE). Sweet Princess, you'll rejoice for the gentleness you have shown me.

FIN. (*to* PEG INERNY). I will call my father up if you don't leave at once. Come, sister, come into the castle.

PEG. Good-night, sweet Maeve—sleep—sleep—and dream. [*Exit at right.*

MA. (*yearningly*). And dream—Oh that I could dream again to-night, that dream!

116

FIN. Don't think of it any more, dearest.   Come in to
rest.

MA. No—let me stay a while longer here.

FIN. But you will be frozen, Maeve.   I wonder you
ever awoke again after falling asleep in the abbey.

MA. Let me stay, Finola, I do not feel the cold.

FIN. It is because you are already so cold.

MA. My love is so divinely cold.

FIN. Ah, that is a strange sort of love.

MA. (*wistfully*). He is the only one I have ever loved.
Let me stay.   I hear him coming.

FIN. (*frightened*). You hear him—?

MA. (*pointing towards the abbey*). Yes, there—far away
—coming on the wings of the March wind.   Don't you
hear ?

FIN. I hear the bitter wind, Maeve, through our old
ash trees.

MA. (*smiling in reverie*). The fairy March wind which
races at twilight over our fields, turning them to that
strange pale beauty, like the beauty of a fairy's face.—Oh,
it is fit that my beloved should ride on such a steed.

FIN. Dearest, you must go to rest.   He will never
come.   He is dead.

MA. He is not dead.   He will come.   I know he will.
But the way is long.   A long—long way.

FIN. A long way, indeed, without beginning and
without end.

MA. It began from the land of everlasting youth.

FIN. You have often told me of that land, Tir-nan-ogue,
is it not ?

MA. The Celtic dream-land of ideal beauty.   There he
lives in never-fading freshness of youth. (*With a steadfast*

visionary look) I am haunted by a boyish face close hooded with short gold hair—and every movement of his slender faultless body goes straight to my heart like a fairy melody. Oh, he has a long way to journey:—for that land of beauty was never so far away as it is to-night.

FIN. (*sadly*). It never was nearer, my poor sister. Come, I will see you to your rest.

MA. I must rest alone, Finola. You must not follow me to my room.

FIN. Why not, dear?

MA. Oh, do not. Leave me to myself.

FIN. (*with a sigh*). Very well, if you wish it.

MA. (*going*). Good-night.

FIN. Good-night, dear.

MA. (*quickly turning and throwing her arms around* FINOLA). Good-night—good-bye—Oh my darling, good-bye.

FIN. (*consolingly*). My poor Maeve, it is not yet the time for parting.

MA. Who knows where I must go, when my beloved shall come.

[*Exit hurriedly by door leading into the Castle.*

FIN. (*wonderingly*). What does she mean by those words? (*With a reassured air*) Oh, she is tired, poor sister. That is what it is. And I suppose her mind is confused with her imaginary difficulties. But all will come well in good time.

[*Exit by door leading into the Castle.* (*Pause.*)

MAEVE O'HEYNES *appears at the window of the castle, above the hall-window facing the right, and slowly opens the casement.*

MA. (*leaning out*). Oh, the beautiful frosty night! I cannot keep it from me. The greatest beauty like the old Greek sculpture is always cold! My Prince of the hoar dew! My golden love, let me see you once more in that aureole of crimson sky! (*With an infinite longing*) Oh that the beauty I saw in my dream could return to me now. (*With sudden terror*) But to-morrow, how shall I face the misery of to-morrow? Oh pity me, pity me— (*Calmer*) And yet I have always known that my beloved would deliver me from bondage. (*With a gradually weaker voice as she sinks upon a chair*) But I am weary of waiting—weary—weary—it is hard to resist the longing for sleep. (*She sighs as she reclines back out of sight in an angle of the window.*) (*Pause.*)

    [*There is a soft music of harps, while the aurora borealis arises and glows in the sky. Soon a ghostly procession is seen to emerge like vapour from the neighbourhood of the cairn. Presently as it advances it grows more distinct and then is discovered to consist of* QUEEN MAEVE, *tall, pale faced and fair haired, in a golden crown and gold embroidered robes; of* BOY PAGES *in garlanded tunics and wearing wreaths of roses upon their heads; of ancient Irish harpers with their harps; of chieftains and warriors in conical caps; of people, etc.*

As they approach near to the castle, MAEVE O'HEYNES *enters from the door at its front, and stands looking on in wonder. They halt; and the harpers cease playing on their harps.*

CHORUS OF BOY PAGES.
(*Singing in broad solemn unison.*)
Every hill which is at this Oenach
Hath under it heroes and Queens,
And poets and distributors,
And fair fierce women.

(*The harpers recommence their music.*)
MA. (*with a thrill of happiness*). Ah, that song of
Dorban I know so well. And this is Queen Maeve again.

(*The harpers cease their music.*)
CHORUS OF BOY PAGES.
Hast seen our warriors? In their hands are white shields
Ornamented with white silver signs—
They wield blue flaming swords
And carry red horns with metal mountings.

MA. (*listening*). Now they are chanting the lay of
Fiachna son of Reta.

A BOY PAGE (*singing alone*).
Obedient to the settled order of the battle,
Preceding their prince of gracious mien
They march across blue lances
Those troops of white warriors with knotted hair.

CHORUS OF BOY PAGES.
They march across blue lances
Those troops of white warriors with knotted hair.

(*The harpers recommence their music.*)
Q. MA. Princess I come, as I have promised.
MA. (*approaching and falling on her knees*). My Queen
—Oh save me, my queen.

Q. Ma. O last of my daughters in the land, what help can I give you?

Ma. My beloved—where is he?

Q. Ma. He is coming over the mountains.   He is coming to you over the mountains.

Ma. (*rising*). Yes, I knew he was coming on the fairy March wind.

Q. Ma. Your love is so great that you divine hi coming? and yet you can suffer bondage?

Ma. How shall I escape the stranger's bondage?

Q. Ma. I will take you to the land of joy.

Ma. To Tir-nan-ogue?—O Queen, do you rule in Tir-nan-ogue?

Q. Ma. The empire of the Gael is in Tir-nan-ogue. There during life he is at peace in the building of beauty from the past.

Ma. And so the land you reign in is the home of living men.

Q. Ma. Each man who comes to his ideal has come to Tir-nan-ogue.

Ma. And thus we see you so young and so beautiful after all those two thousand years!

Q. Ma. Your fame also shall remain beautiful and young.

Ma. Of what kind is the happiness that makes Tir-nan-ogue happy?

Q. Ma. Happiness in the present as sweet as the remembrance of happiness.

Ma. Then shall my happiness be great indeed.

Q. Ma. You remember much happiness?

Ma. I remember beauty.

Q. Ma. Those who love beauty shall see beauty.

121

MA. The immortal beauty of form!

Q. MA. Form that will awaken genius!

MA. Form is my beauty and my love!

(*The harpers cease their music.*)

CHORUS OF BOY PAGES.

Their strength, great as it is, can not be less,
They are sons of queens and kings,
On the heads of all a comely
Growth of hair yellow like gold.

A BOY PAGE.

Their bodies are graceful and majestic,
Their eyes with a look of power have the eye-ball blue.
Their teeth are brilliant like glass,
Their lips are red and thin.

CHORUS OF BOY PAGES.

Their bodies are graceful and majestic,
These sons of queens and kings.

(*The harpers recommence their music.*)

MA. So Fiachna is made to sing when the poet tells how the hero came from the land of the gods. I love that poem!

Q. MA. I have all the poems — the greatest those that are lost. Come into my land; and they that made them shall sing them, and their music shall turn all things to beauty.

MA. Queen, I have seen that land afar.

Q. MA. You also have seen Tir-nan-ogue?

MA. In my dreams, in my day-dreams.

Q. MA. Daughter, it is passing sweet when our day-dreams come true.

MA. Oh let me see the beloved of my day-dreams.

Q. MA. Your Prince of the hoar dew, when he comes, will give you rest.

MA. Rest without pain or fear of bondage?

Q. MA. Rest in beauty—a beauty which is transcendently cold.

MA. Oh let me see that beauty. I have sought it in vain on earth.

Q. MA. He is coming, he is coming over the mountains. You shall speak to him when he is come.

MA. (*with a sudden disconsolate look*). I will never speak to him.

Q. MA. Why, wayward child?

MA. Queen, I cannot. The sight of such beauty will make me speechless.

Q. MA. Then shall you find peace in his beauty.

MA. But oh, my queen, let me see him.

Q. MA. You shall see him in the Northern lights of Tir-nan-ogue.

MA. And his beauty shall be my joy in an ideal land.

Q. MA. Beauty in the midst of all beautiful things.

MA. Oh take me to that land.

Q. MA. I am waiting for you, poor weary child.

MA. The land where my day-dreams will come true!

Q. MA. See, the Northern lights are passing before the dawn. We must not tarry.

MA. I am ready, my beautiful queen.

Q. MA. Then come with the Northern lights, beautiful ice maiden!

MA. I shall see my beauty—my love—!

(*Half swooning she falls on the neck of* QUEEN MAEVE.)
    (*The harpers cease their music.*)

Noble and melodious music thou dost hear;
Thou goest from kingdom to kingdom
Drinking from goblets of massy gold,
Thou wilt discourse with thy beloved.

A BOY PAGE.

We have carried from the plain Mag Mell
Thirty caldrons, thirty horns for drinking
We have carried from it the lamentation sung by Mear,
Daughter of Eochaid the Dumb.

(*The harpers re-commence their music.*)

CHORUS OF BOY PAGES.

What a marvel in Tir-nan-ogue
That mead should fall with each shower,
Drinking from goblets of massy gold,
Thou wilt discourse with thy beloved.

[*During this song all, including* MAEVE O'HEYNES,
*have gradually moved off towards the cairn and
faded away with the aurora borealis, so that, when
the music ceases, no trace of them remains. A faint
grey light of dawn now prevails; and then the whole
scene, at the approach of sunrise, is discovered to be
completely white with a thick coating of hoar frost.*

After a while HUGH FITZ WALTER, *muffled and carrying
a large bunch of flowers, enters from the left.*

HUGH. I can wait no longer. I must come to her
castle with the first light. How fine it looks decked
out with the hoar frost! Oh, I hope she is safe and well;
let these be my morning offering before she awakes. (*He
lays the flowers by the doorway of the castle.*)

124

The O'HEYNES, *also muffled, enters from the left.*

THE O'H. (*looking in the direction of* HUGH). Ah! you too, are out early this morning.

HUGH. Yes. Somehow I felt I had to come.

THE O'H. What a blessing you are here at last, Hugh. (*He grasps him by the hand.*)

HUGH. I wish I could have returned sooner.

THE O'H. I wish you could have. Well, let that be.

HUGH. But why are you also about at this hour of the morning? I did not expect to see any one stirring.

THE O'H. (*peevishly*). I could not sleep these hours past with thinking and thinking. Then something made me get up, and see what would happen.

HUGH. (*anxiously*). What would happen? Heavens! what do you expect to happen?

THE O'H. Oh nothing, nothing, I suppose. Only my mind will not let me rest.

HUGH. Do you know I too was very uneasy about things last night.

THE O'H. (*suspiciously*). You, why? What reason could you have had?

HUGH. (*with rather a forced laugh*). Oh, none of course. How could I?

THE O'H. Of course not—of course not. But come in to the fire, Hugh, and warm yourself. There has been a great frost last night.

HUGH. Yes, the whole country is white, as if it were covered with snow.

THE O'H. A March frost soon melts before the sun. See, it is already rising. The day is going to be a glorious one.

HUGH. There is an old saying—"Happy is the bride the sun shines on."

As they go towards the door of the castle,
FINOLA O'HEYNES *enters from it.*

FIN. Oh, what lovely flowers!

HUGH. I brought them for Maeve. She is not yet awake?

FIN. No. I gave orders she was not to be disturbed. It was very late last night when she went to rest; and she seemed so tired.

HUGH. Then I would not have her disturbed for worlds. Will you bring her these flowers, Finola, when she awakes?

PEG INERNY *enters from the right.*

PEG. When she awakes—? Ah,—my Princess Maeve —do you think she will care for such flowers now?

HUGH (*in a subdued voice*). Why not? Why do you say she would not?

PEG. Oh, it's a cold morning, a cruel cold morning.

FIN. Go away from this place.—Let me never see you again.

PEG. I have never before been refused the shelter of O'Heynes Castle.

HUGH. O'Heynes Castle is never the better for your presence. I understand you are always importuning Miss O'Heynes.

THE O'H. Come, we must not be hard to the old woman on such a day as this. Go round to the kitchen, Peg, and get something to eat.

PEG. Yes, some food. I want some food and warmth, Prince—I have been out all night, and I am famished.

THE O'H. Well, then, get all you wish. The Castle

hall is open to everyone in honour of my daughters' wedding to-day.

HUGH. Yes, we must try to make everyone happy to-day—even this wicked old woman.

PEG (*with a sinister look*). I suppose you also, my brave Englishman, think you ought to be happy.

HUGH. Why—of course. Don't you know I am to be married to-day?

PEG (*almost contemptuously*). You married to the Princess Maeve?

HUGH (*bridling up*). Yes.

PEG (*mockingly*). Well, well, how queer that you should think so!

FIN. (*with a scared expression*). There is misfortune in those words.

THE O'H. Peg Inerny, you are awakening my forebodings again.

PEG (*humbly*). Oh, Prince, I can't say otherwise.

HUGH (*indignantly*). What old woman's talk is this?

PEG (*with a quiet prophetic triumph*). You think I am only an old woman; but I tell you that Erin can never be subdued.

HUGH. I should like to know what that has to do with the matter?

PEG (*smiling insidiously*). Perhaps the Englishman may think that he already holds her? Ah, she will slip like a fairy from his grasp. (*She laughs low and sardonically.*)

FIN. (*excitedly to* PEG INERNY). Leave the place at once, you wicked woman. Oh, drive her away, Hugh, before she says any more.

HUGH (*advances to* PEG INERNY, *who draws herself*

up defiantly. He then steps back, saying, with a forced laugh) What do I care for her.   I shall soon be married and far away!

PEG. Take care, my fine Englishman, if your Irish Princess hasn't already slipped from you like a fairy.

THE O'H (*nervously*). What do you mean, Peg Inerny?

PEG. Oh, my Prince, just before dawn upon the mountains—I saw her.

HUGH (*with a look of terror*). You saw her?

PEG (*with a smile of ecstacy*). Yes, I saw my Princess Maeve!

HUGH (*turning perplexed to* THE O'HEYNES *and to* FINOLA).   But—but didn't you say she was there in the castle?

THE O'H. (*with a helpless look*). I thought so.   I am sure I thought so.   Didn't you say she was here, Finola?

FIN. (*in a hollow voice*). Yes, father. (*As if petrified she now slowly retreats towards the castle door, keeping her eyes always fixed on* PEG INERNY.)

HUGH. Oh that Maeve should be wandering over the mountains on such a night as this.

THE O'H. (*confusedly*). I knew some misfortune was coming.   What has happened?

PEG (*with increasing ecstacy*). If you had only seen her, as I saw her upon the mountain—she was so beautiful—so happy.   You would have died at the sight of such beauty, my Englishman.

HUGH (*with a look of bitterness and despair*). As if I required to be persuaded of her beauty!

PEG (*quietly*). And you will never see it again.

[*Exit* FINOLA O'HEYNES *by door leading into the castle.*

MAEVE

HUGH (*suddenly subdued*). Never again—why never again?

PEG. It has gone to where he is.

HUGH (*wildly*). He—he—who is he? Speak at once. Don't you see you torture me?

PEG. The beauty that she loves.

HUGH (*growing quieter*). Ah, I understand—only that.

PEG (*calmly triumphant and ecstatic*). Like the glory of the Northern lights was his face upon the mountains. And when she saw him, her own face shone like a star.

HUGH (*as if transfixed*). Oh what does all this mean? (*Recovering himself*) Ha—ha—it is nothing. Of course you are only raving. That's what it is. Anyone can see that.

THE O'H. (*with an agonised look*). She has given utterance to my worst forebodings. Tell what you saw next, Peg Inerny.

PEG. The dawn came then; and Princess Maeve went out from my sight with the stars!

(*Short pause.*)

(*Cries of "help" are heard within the Castle. Then* FINOLA O'HEYNES, *with a scared face, appears at the window over the entrance door, and throws the casement open violently*).

FIN. (*wailing*). Oh heavens, oh, my heavens—oh— (*looks across the room towards the window facing the abbey at right, and after a moment's awful silence says in a voice of terror*)—Maeve—she is sitting there at the open window—dead.

THE END.

PRINTED BY
TURNBULL AND SPEARS,
EDINBURGH

MODERN PLAYS.

Edited by R. Brimley Johnson and N. Erichsen.

It is the aim of this series to represent, as widely as possible, the activity of the modern drama—not confined to stage performance—in England and throughout the continent of Europe. It so happens that, though translations seem to be more in demand every day, the greater number of the Continental dramatists are at present little known in this country. Among them will be found predecessors and followers of Ibsen or Maeterlinck; as well as others who reflect more independently the genius of their own country.

Love's Comedy, which marks a transition from the early romantic to the later social plays, is the only important work of Ibsen's not yet translated into English. The name of Strindberg, whose position in Sweden may be compared to that of Ibsen in Norway, will be almost new to the English public. Villiers' *La Révolte* is a striking forecast of *The Doll's House*. Verhaeren is already known here as one of the foremost of Belgian writers, who, like Maeterlinck, uses the French tongue; and Brieux is among the most attractive of the younger native French dramatists. Ostrovsky's *The Storm*, painting "The Dark World," is generally recognised as *the* characteristic Russian drama. *The Convert*, by Stepniak, will be specially interesting as its author's only dramatic attempt.

The work of translation has been entrusted to English writers specially conversant with the literatures represented, who, in many cases, are already associated in the public mind with the authors they are here interpreting. Every play will be translated *in extenso*, and, if in verse, as nearly as possible in the original metres. The volumes will contain brief introductions, bibliographical and explanatory rather than critical, and such annotations as may be necessary.

The volumes will be printed in pott quarto, and they will cost, as a rule, 2s. 6d. net. or 3s. 6d. net. each.

EARLY VOLUMES.

EMILE VERHAEREN
 "Les Aubes " (" The Dawn ").—ARTHUR SYMONS.

OSTROVSKY
 " The Storm."—CONSTANCE GARNETT.

MAURICE MAETERLINCK
 " Intérieur."—WILLIAM ARCHER.
 " La Mort de Tintagiles." ⎫
 " Alladine et Palomides." ⎭ —ALFRED SUTRO.

HENRIK IBSEN
 "Love's Comedy" (*Kjærlighedens Komedie*).—Prof. C. H. HERFORD.

VILLIERS DE L'ISLE ADAM
 " La Révolte." ⎫
 " L'Evasion." ⎭ —THERESA BARCLAY.

SERGIUS STEPNIAK
 " The Convert."—CONSTANCE GARNETT.

AUGUST STRINDBERG
 " The Father " (*Fadren*).—N. ERICHSEN.

BRIEUX
 " Les Bienfaiteurs."—LUCAS MALET.

HENRYK SIENKIEWICZ
 "On a Single Card."—E. L. VOYNICH.

Arrangements are also in progress with representative dramatists of Germany, Spain, Italy, and other countries. Further translations have been promised by Dr GARNETT, Messrs WALTER LEAF, JUSTIN HUNTLY MACCARTHY, G. A. GREENE, &c.